When I reached the top, I thought I felt something flying above me, circling the spot where I stood. I looked up, but there was nothing other than snow. As soon as I put my head down, I felt it again. I thought I caught a glimpse of something that was shining this time. I waved my arms above my head. Could it be one of my angels?

"Aurora, is that you?" I called.

There was no reply.

All I could see was a wall of white everywhere I turned. What good would it do to yell for help? What good would it do to stand still and wait? What good would it do to move on? Now I was feeling really helpless. Even worse, my hands and feet were becoming numb from the cold.

"Angels!" I whispered, burying my face in the fur of my hood. "Please come and help me!"

Hannah and the Angels
Trouble on Ice

by Linda Lowery Keep

Based on a concept by
Linda Lowery Keep
and Carole Newhouse

Random House 🏠 New York

For the <u>Tapirisat</u> involved in <u>Hannah and the Angels</u>: the readers, the production staff, and, of course, the angels. The more curious we all are about the rich cultures of our world, the more we build a united and exciting team together on this planet.

Acknowledgments

Thank you and *qujannamiik* to Looee Okalik of the Inuit Tapirisat of Canada in Ottawa, Ontario, for her patient help in teaching me to pronounce and spell the Inuktitut words Hannah learned on her adventure. Her name, Okalik, by the way, means "Arctic hare." *Tapirisat* means "team builders."

Thank you and "woof" to Donald Dodge, D.V.M., for his expert veterinary advice about the dangers of antifreeze and the care and healing of animals.

Contents

1. Chasing My Tail   1
2. Snow Angel   5
3. Ee-nook-sook   13
4. The Mighty Nanuks   22
5. Mission: Rescue!   27
6. Santa's Little Reindeer   33
7. Who's the Boss?   39
8. Lemming Land   44
9. Ice Palace   48
10. Blubber for Supper   55
11. Poison Pawprints   62
12. Aurora Borealis   68
13. Skunk Muffin   73
14. Husky Hospital   78
15. Fireworks in the Sky   83
16. Angels, Angels Everywhere   88
17. Ukpik   92
18. Some Sleepover!   97
19. New Babies   102

Hannah and the Angels

Trouble on Ice

Chapter 1

Chasing My Tail

My dog, Frank, is just like me—he needs *adventure*. When he's stuck in one place for too long, he gets all weird and starts chasing his tail. For

Frank, chasing his tail

instance, it flurried a few days ago, so Frank began curiously sniffing around. When the snow kept coming and he realized he couldn't go outside because it was too cold, Frank hid under the dining room table and pouted. Finally, when Wednesday came and it was still snowing, he couldn't think of anything to do but chase his tail. No adventure, no fun.

If I had a tail, I would have chased it by now, too. You see, all this snow has shut down school. Now, don't get me wrong—I *love* snow days. Nothing could be better than no school. And at

1

first, I was having a lot of fun. I spent two days piecing together a scrapbook of all my angel trips. Here, I'll show you:

First, I put in a drawing of me, Hannah Martin, with all four of my angels: Aurora, Lyra, Lorielle, and Demetriel. Then I put in pictures of all the great friends I'd met. I put in the song I wrote on my foot in Trinidad and a photo of Molly by a gravestone in Ireland. Under "Strange and Amazing Stuff," I put Australian words and the medicine man from Kenya. And I pasted in Frankie's calypso valentine at the end. (Actually, it's not the end—there are lots of blank pages left for future angel trips I don't even know about yet.)

Some scrapbook pictures

After I finished my scrapbook, I hid it inside my window seat (just to be safe—my mom and dad would *never* understand my angel trips). Then I flipped through about twelve magazines, baked chocolate chip cookies, rearranged my Pez collection, trimmed my split ends, read a book, watched way too much TV, and shoveled snow. I couldn't think of anything else to do. Since my best friends, Katie and David, were out of town, I thought maybe it was time to start chasing *my* imaginary tail.

"Why don't you get outside?" my mother suggested. She'd been perfectly content to sit at the computer doing her work for the past two days. I guess my pacing around was beginning to drive her crazy.

I decided that a hike to the lake would do me some good. It was frozen solid under the snow, so maybe I could slide around on the ice. I packed as if I was going on a real trip. I took all my school stuff out of my backpack, and I threw in six cookies I'd baked, two oranges, and a water bottle. I added a compass and flashlight (in case I dug a massive snow tunnel), my journal, and my flute. I wiggled into my long underwear, double-layered my sweatshirts, and pulled on my ski bibs. For good measure, I stuck two heating packets in my boots to keep my toes warm. I bundled up until I looked like a stuffed sausage in a ski suit.

Stuffed in my ski suit

"Bye, Mom!" I called.

My mother sighed with relief. "I'm glad you're getting some exercise," she called back. "Have fun!"

Just to be dramatic, I scribbled a note to my dad, who was out on an emergency veterinarian call. He'd actually cross-country-skied way across town through the snow because somebody's dog was about to have puppies.

Dear Dad,
  I'm going on a snowy adventure.
  I hope I'll come back with interesting stories to tell.
  See you later.

                              Love,
                           S. Muffin

The "S" stands for Skunk. My dad has lots of goofy nicknames for me. Lately, he's been calling me Skunk Muffin. He thinks it's cute. I guess it's just my dad's vet humor.

Anyway, I set out on my excursion in the snow. Little did I know it would turn out to be a major adventure, far beyond a simple winter hike through my Geneva, Wisconsin, neighborhood.

Chapter 2

Snow Angel

I lumbered down my street through the deep snow like the Abominable Snowman. All the homes looked like frosted gingerbread houses with snowy icing piled on the roofs. It was early afternoon, so I had plenty of time to head to the lake. When I finally arrived, it looked like an untouched field of ice and snow—except where

My house

Katie and David's house

To the lake ⟶

people were ice fishing. The ice fishermen had driven way out, had set up their shacks, and were fishing through holes in the frozen lake. I always have thought that if enough people turned on the heaters in their shacks at the same time, there'd be one major meltdown. The ice would crack, cars would sink, and people would plunge down into the freezing-cold water. Well, it's never happened yet, so I guess I didn't have to worry about it.

The rest of the lake looked like a huge snow blanket. I hiked out to a perfect spot to make a snow angel. I lay down and started waving my arms to make wings. I swished my legs out and back to make a long skirt. Then I closed my eyes and felt the snowflakes fall on my eyelashes. They felt light and magical, like stardust. I lay there and listened to the silence. It was so quiet that I could hear my heart thumping.

Thump! Thump! Thump!

Wait a minute. Is that really my heartbeat? I thought. How could it be beating that loud? It sounded more like a drumbeat than anything else. Then I realized it wasn't my heart after all. It was some kind of actual drum that was getting louder and louder, beating in my ears. I opened my eyes and looked up at the falling snow through...a ring of fur?

Weird!

Fur was all around my face on a hood that I hadn't been wearing when I had lain down just a few seconds ago. The drum beating had stopped, but I realized that it was sunset *already!* I tried to leap to my feet, but there were big, clunky tennis rackets strapped onto my boots. And my clothes were heavier than before. I still had on my ski bibs, but now I was wearing a bulky jacket and thick mittens!

Did I just get transported on an angel mission? I thought to myself. I stood on the stomach of my snow angel and looked all around. Snow was everywhere. In fact, that was all I could see. The first thing I felt was terror. Was I where the *real* Abominable Snowman lurked? Were there wolves here? Or polar bears? Or wolves *and* polar bears? I took a long, frosty breath. I never thought my angels would send me to a dangerous place like this. But I figured that wherever I was, I was here for a reason.

I didn't know what to do next, so I decided to yell.

"Hellooooo! Is anybody out there?" My voice didn't travel far because the snow cushioned the sound. It was like hollering in a padded room. Now I was scared *and* lonely. I tried yelling a few more times. When that didn't work, I figured I better start walking. But in which direction?

I set my backpack down to grab my compass and just happened to see my snow angel from the corner of my eye. Her arm suddenly moved! It was now pointing up above her head. I knew it

was my angel Aurora at
work. She's the angel
in charge, and she
always sends me
messages with signs
from nature. Before I
headed off in the
direction Aurora was
pointing, I decided
to check my back-

My snow angel, pointing east

pack first. My angels always put some neat stuff
in there for my missions.

I took off my mittens to open the flap and my
fingers nearly froze immediately. As soon as I got

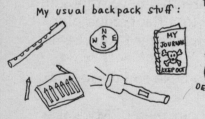

My usual backpack stuff:

ANGEL
DECODER

the flap undone, I pulled
my mittens back on and
checked through my
stuff. Everything I'd
packed before was
still in there, plus a
telescope and a star
map. The snow was filling up my pack so fast
that my journal was getting all
soaked. I fished out my compass, closed up my pack
(before seeing if my angels
had left anything else
inside), and started out in
the direction my snow

Special supplies

star chart

telescope

(glow-in-the-dark)

angel's hand pointed to. According to the compass, I was heading east.

The "tennis rackets" on my feet were very handy. It didn't take me too long to figure out they were actually snowshoes. I'd pick up a foot and set it down, and instead of my leg dropping all the way down into a snow hole, the shoes kind of lifted me up and kept me more on top of the surface. Very cool!

snowshoes

I began to feel like an Arctic explorer. Maybe I was discovering some frigid land nobody had ever seen before. Or on second thought, maybe somebody *had* walked this landscape before and had frozen to death or gotten slashed by a polar bear. Thinking about freezing and polar bears started to freak me out, so I decided to calm myself down.

You can survive anything, I told myself. I continued trudging along, looking for anything besides snow. An igloo? A cozy log cabin with a blazing fire? Anything.

It started to become darker and colder. The night was taking the heat from the sun minute by minute. I pulled the strings on my hood really tight so all I could see was a long, narrow tunnel leading to a tiny opening of snow. Pretty soon, the snow was swirling around me like a tornado, with me as the center. That's when I realized I was in the middle of a whiteout! Everything was pitch-dark, snowy, and freezing cold.

My snowshoes weren't fun anymore—it had become hard work marching through the deep snow. I breathed into the fur of my hood to keep my face warm. That's when the bear thoughts totally overtook me.

Isn't this the kind of place where those ferocious Kodiak bears live? I thought to myself. *The bears who can track people down for hundreds of miles by following their scent? The bears that can smell your scent even in a blizzard?* Now I was *really* freaking myself out. All I could think about was how I was oozing some pungent humanoid odor the way that skunks discharge their skunky smell.

The more I pictured bear claws and teeth, the faster I tried to walk. The edges of the snowshoes were catching in the drifts, and I lost my balance.

Thump!

I was on the ground deep in blankets of snow. Every time I tried to get up, I fell over like a big snowman. I couldn't get any leverage with my arms because they just sank deeper into the snow. What was I going to do? Crying wouldn't help— my tears would freeze on my face and probably leave permanent ruts.

As scared as I was, I knew I had to stay calm and not have a panic attack. I needed to form a plan. I suddenly thought about camping with my dad. I tried to remember all the stuff he had told me to do if I ever got lost. I listed his advice in my head, as if I was writing in my journal.

* * *

1. Hug a tree and wait for someone to find you.

What tree? There were zero trees anywhere. I figured I must be in the tundra or something. And if I wait for somebody to find me, I thought, it will be spring and I'll be a pile of bones with snowshoes strapped on my feet.

2. Build a fire and drink some hot tea with cayenne pepper to warm your body.

Oh, right! That'll work. No wood, no matches, and two tons of snow falling every second! All I have to burn for fuel is my journal—and I could never do that!

3. If no one comes to find you, climb a hill and look around.

Even if I found a hill, I wouldn't be able to see a thing through this snow. Besides, how do you find a hill in a whiteout?

Not one bit of Dad's camping advice would work. But as I had been concentrating on other problems, I had somehow solved the puzzle of getting back on my feet. I was standing up again! Maybe if I stopped struggling and kept walking slowly, at least I wouldn't end up buried in six feet of snow. Soon I was making my way up a hill. *Okay, that is good,* I told myself. *Up is better than down.*

When I reached the top, I thought I felt something flying above me, circling the spot where I stood. I looked up, but there was nothing other than snow. As soon as I put my head down, I felt it again. I thought I caught a glimpse of something that was shining this time. I waved my arms above my head. Could it be one of my angels?

"Aurora, is that you?" I called.

There was no reply.

All I could see was a wall of white everywhere I turned. What good would it do to yell for help? What good would it do to stand still and wait? What good would it do to move on? I was feeling really helpless. Even worse, my hands and feet were becoming numb from the cold.

"Angels!" I whispered, burying my face in the fur of my hood. "Please come help me!"

Chapter 3

Eee-nook-sook

When I pulled my nose from the fur lining and peered out, I saw a dark shape moving in the swirling snow. It wasn't flying over my head. Instead, it was lumbering toward me like a bear. I stood dead still.

"Hey, Hannah!" a deep voice called.

I quickly decided that it was either a man or a mirage of a talking bear. I'd read about how Arctic explorers saw visions the way people see water in the desert when they're hallucinating from sunstroke. I squinted through my furry tunnel.

Soon, someone really did emerge in the snow. And it was a human, thank goodness. In a fur hood and heavy clothes, this person looked just like me—except a lot bigger. I was so glad to have somebody else out there. The person nodded and motioned for me to follow. Everything seemed as if it was in slow motion.

"Who are you?" I called.

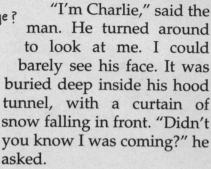

Was it real or was it a mirage?

"I'm Charlie," said the man. He turned around to look at me. I could barely see his face. It was buried deep inside his hood tunnel, with a curtain of snow falling in front. "Didn't you know I was coming?" he asked.

"Uh...no," I stammered. This was so weird! He was acting like he'd come to pick me up from the airport or something—like it was no big deal we were in the middle of a whiteout!

"How did you know my name?" I asked.

"I was expecting you," he said.

"You *were?*" I asked, amazed. "Who told you I'd be here?" Maybe my angels had sent him a message.

Charlie shook his head like it wasn't important. "Come on, let's get out of the snow," he said. I was going to ask him if he had seen a shining object flying around in the storm, but it didn't seem like the right time.

My legs were so tired that they were quivering

with every step. I decided to follow behind him. I noticed that Charlie walked really slow—I guess that's the best way to keep your balance in snowshoes. It wasn't far at all before I began to see the lights from some buildings. If it hadn't been for the blizzard, I probably would have seen the town from where I landed.

We arrived at a concrete building. As we walked inside, I noticed a bunch of snowshoes and parkas hanging from pegs. It looked like the entrance to a school gym. I heard a lot of rowdy shouting coming from inside. Charlie shook off all the snow and unfastened his jacket. I did the same.

"So you have something to do with dogs and kids in trouble, huh?" he asked while I unstrapped my snowshoes. I could see his face now—it was brown, like a deep, wrinkled tan. His hair was graying and pulled back into a ponytail.

"Uh...I have no idea," I answered.

He smiled and nodded, as if I had answered yes. "I'll introduce you around," he said.

"Charlie, where am I?" I asked.

"Inuksuk," he said. It sounded to me like Eee-nook-sook. Charlie could tell by my blank look that I'd never heard of it. "Baffin Island," he added.

He looked at me again. I was as blank as ever. "Nunavut—our new territory? Hudson Bay?" he asked to see if anything would ring a bell with me. "Canada?"

"Oh, okay!" I said. Well, I certainly knew where Canada was. And Hudson Bay was where the pioneers traded beads with the Indians to get furs. My friend David had told me how the beads were worthless but the furs were very valuable. A big rip-off, right?

"Make yourself at home, Hannah," Charlie said. "We have a couple of hours before the big game starts."

Big game? Did my mission have something to do with some sort of game?

I opened the door Charlie motioned to. There were volleyballs and basketballs lying all over the place. Kids were laughing and shouting. Some of them were shooting hoops, some were kicking balls around, and some were just racing around. It *was* a school gym after all. There were only about twenty kids, but their voices were bouncing off the walls, so it sounded like a hundred.

"Hey, Laurel!" Charlie called to one of them. "How about welcoming our visitor here? Her name is Hannah."

An older girl with a fringed shirt and glasses came over to shake my hand. "Hey, Hannah," she said. "Have you ever been on a trampoline before?"

"Sure," I said.

"Then you've got to try out the blanket toss."

"Okay," I said.

Laurel looked down at my feet. "First, you've got to take off those boots," she said. "Come here." She reached under the wooden bench, grabbed some shoes, and held them up for me to choose. "Gym shoes or *kamiik?*" she asked.

I pointed to the soft leather boots with the beaded trim. "I'll take those," I said. They looked a lot warmer—and warm was definitely what I needed. Besides, they looked like something an Arctic explorer would wear.

"*Kamiik* is a nice word," I said as I pulled them on. They were *really* comfy. As we headed toward the blanket toss, I asked Laurel about Charlie. I wanted to know how he knew I was stuck in the snow.

The boots are called kamiik

"Charlie's a great guy," Laurel told me. "Where I come from in Canada, some people might call him a little...spooky. He runs the post office, and he's also our resident medicine man. He knows everybody in town."

"Charlie's a medicine man?" I asked. I'd met a medicine man on my angel trip to Kenya. He was all exotic-looking, with beads, a red robe, and bags of secret stones. Charlie just looked like a regular guy in jeans and a sweatshirt.

"In the old days," explained Laurel, "people like Charlie were called *angakkuit.*" It sounded like on-guh-queet. Laurel went on, "People say they had special powers and could shape-shift."

"Shape-shift?" I asked.

"You know, they could turn into ravens, or foxes, or polar bears."

I looked over at Charlie and tried to imagine him turning into an animal.

"Charlie can't really shape-shift, can he?" I whispered.

"I couldn't say," Laurel answered, looking away from me.

"But if he's a medicine man, does he heal sick people?" I asked.

"Sometimes," said Laurel.

"What else does he do?" I asked. As you can tell, I'm a very curious person. I think it's to feed my imagination. Before I could stop myself, my brain was already concocting a story about Charlie the magic shape-shifter.

"Well, sometimes he knows things that happen before you see it on the news or read it in the paper," said Laurel. "Anyway, Charlie's a great guy, no matter what." Then Laurel turned away from me and faced the kids who were kicking a ball that was dangling from a basketball hoop.

I felt a quick little tug on my hair and spun around. Nobody was there, so I knew right away it was an angel tug. I quickly faced the wall so nobody could hear me having a conversation with an invisible friend. (That doesn't exactly make for good first impressions!)

"Demi?" I whispered. "Demi" is short for "Demetriel"—she's my angel who tries to keep me in line. As usual, she was hovering around me somewhere. I didn't hear an answer, but I *felt* one. I could tell Demi was warning me to quit asking so many questions about Charlie. Sometimes I get a bit too nosy for my own good.

I looked back at Laurel. She still had her back turned to me. I decided to take Demi's advice, and I changed the subject.

"What are those kids doing?" I asked her.

"That's the one-foot high kick," she said. "It's an Inuit game."

"An Ee-new-eet game?" I asked.

Laurel looked at me strangely. "Where are you from, Hannah?" she asked. "You sure don't seem to know much."

"I'm...ummm...I'm from Wisconsin," I answered.

"I'm from Quebec," she said. "I'm part Inuit, but I've always lived around Canadians who aren't Inuit. So I'm up here studying my culture. I'm also working as a nurse."

"So tell me about the Inuit games," I said, trying to keep the conversation simple.

Laurel wasn't letting me off the hook that easily, though. "You came two thousand miles for a kids' basketball tournament?"

A basketball tournament?

"Not exactly," I quickly said. "I'm very interested in Inuit culture, too." What a ridiculous fib that was.

"Well, you came to the right place," said Laurel. "Most of the people on Baffin Island are Inuit. They're natives, which means they're the original people who have always lived here."

"That must be the Inuit blanket toss game," I said, pointing to some kids who were holding a huge blanket by rope handles and tossing a boy high in the air. Everybody was screaming and laughing.

blanket
toss

"That's right," said Laurel. We walked toward the blanket toss.

"There aren't too many kids here so far," said Laurel. "The storm's really bad."

"I noticed," I said.

"The semi-finals are a *big* deal. The other team, the Kodiaks, are flying in. But with this weather, we're afraid they might have to turn around and fly back home."

"A basketball team is taking a *plane* to get here for a game?" I asked, astonished. "Our teams just take buses in Wisconsin."

Laurel laughed. "Isn't it weird? We take buses in Quebec, too. But up here, sometimes there aren't even roads between towns. You have to take planes to get around." I couldn't imagine living in a place that was so far from other towns. And I thought it took a long time to get to Grandma Zoe's house!

"Come on, Hannah. Are you ready to get tossed?" Laurel asked.

Of course I was ready to get tossed! I'm always up for a new fling.

"Everybody, this is Hannah," yelled Laurel. She told me the names of all the kids, really fast, so I forgot half of them. There was Cody, Adam, Peter, Mary, and a girl named Malila (whose name, Laurel said, means "salmon swimming fast upstream"). That's all the names I could remember.

"Hi, everybody," I said.

Next thing I knew, I was in the middle of the blanket, and all the kids were throwing me into the air. They went easy on me at first, but soon I was rushing toward the ceiling, as if I'd been catapulted out of a cannon. A big sign hanging on the wall seemed to fly past my face. It said:

Chapter 4

The Mighty Nanuks

After I got over the initial terror, I decided that it was a lot of fun to be tossed. I started pirouetting in circles and kicking my legs, as if I was walking on air. I was screaming like everybody else, and it felt good. It's like when you scream on a roller coaster or in a haunted house. If you're silent, you're terrified. But if you scream, you feel better.

"How much can you see from up there?" Laurel called to me.

"Everything!" I shouted. "I can see everything!"

They told me this was the way Inuit scouts used to look out for animals or enemies up ahead on the flat tundra. The group would toss the scout really high, and he could see for miles around. It really worked—I could see everything in the gym, including a very tall man strutting through the door.

"Whoa, Nellie!" the tall man shouted, looking up at me. His voice boomed and echoed throughout the gym. "I believe there's a kid that I've never seen before flying in the air."

"Hey, it's Bly!" someone hollered. Half the kids ran to see him. Our blanket toss came to a swift halt. I stumbled off the blanket onto the floor all sweaty and dizzy.

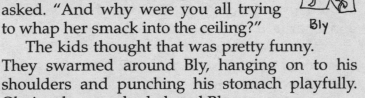

Bly

"So who's the stranger, eh?" Bly asked. "And why were you all trying to whap her smack into the ceiling?"

The kids thought that was pretty funny. They swarmed around Bly, hanging on to his shoulders and punching his stomach playfully. Obviously, everybody loved Bly.

"That's Hannah," Charlie said. "She came a long way to see the game tonight."

"Hannah Banana? Why, hello!" Bly bellowed as he greeted me across the pile of kids. As I waved back, I noticed he was wearing a cowboy hat, a shirt with big yellow and purple flowers blooming on it, and a Hawaiian lei around his neck. His hat and *kamiiks* still had patches of frozen snow on them.

"Sorry, guys! I didn't bring any supplies for you today," he told the kids. "I'm just lucky I landed okay in this whiteout."

"No CDs, Coach?" asked Cody.

"No new videos?" Mary whined.

"When I say no supplies, I mean *nada*, bean-heads! Zilch!" Bly boomed. "I'll have some good stuff next time, though. Now, in the meantime, let's get busy. We've got a game to play!"

He clapped his hands together. It was so loud that it sounded like thunder.

"Why aren't you guys suited up?" he asked. "Let's move! *Atii!*" (He pronounced it Ah-tee. From the way everybody scrambled, I figured it must mean "Let's go!") Laurel and I didn't have anywhere to go, so we just stood there with Bly and Charlie.

"We weren't sure if the Kodiaks would get weathered out," Charlie told Bly. "I've got a bad feeling about this storm."

Suddenly, Bly looked very serious. "It turned wicked out there real fast, Charlie," he said. "I heard on my radio coming in that a plane went down up north. The rescue squad's on its way up there right now."

Laurel's eyes got huge. "It's not the Kodiaks' plane, is it?" she asked nervously.

"No, no," said Bly. "It's a man and his wife who were probably on their way to Iqaluit. They crashed a few miles north of town."

Charlie and Bly then started talking in a different language.

"They're speaking Inuktitut," Laurel told me.

(It's pronounced Eee-nook-tee-toot.)

"Can you understand them?" I asked. I hate being left out of a conversation just because I don't speak the language. It kind of makes me impatient.

"I can't understand much," said Laurel. "I speak French and English. I'm just learning Inuktitut. They're saying something about the Kodiak kids."

Just then, Bly and Charlie switched back to English.

"Have they been in radio contact?" asked Charlie.

Bly nodded. "Yes. Last time I heard, the pilot was trying to decide whether it's safer to turn back or keep going."

"That's what I thought," said Charlie. "How about I see what I can pick up on the radio while you get warm-ups started?"

"Sure thing," said Bly. He turned to me and Laurel. "Don't say a word to the kids, you hear?" he warned sternly. "I don't want anybody to start panicking."

We both nodded.

The team trotted back into the gym and began their stretching. Then they formed two lines and practiced lay-ups. Bly pulled off his heavy leggings to sport his coaching shorts—fluorescent orange with green palm trees. He walked to the middle of the court and blew his whistle.

"Are the Kodiaks going to make it?" asked Cody.

"We don't know yet," said Bly. "But that has nothing to do with our practice. C'mon, I want to see you guys play some tough ball. *Atii*, Mighty Nanuks!"

As I watched Bly jogging around in his Hawaiian duds coaching the team, all I could think about was the storm and the plane full of Kodiak kids. Just like Charlie had said, I knew my mission had something to do with them.

I thought about how scared I'd been out in the blizzard just a while ago. But at least my feet had been on the ground. To actually be flying in a plane through this weather would be the worst ever. Definitely *not* a cool situation.

Then I had a bad thought: I had no idea how weather affects angels. Was it dangerous for them to fly in a blizzard, too? Would they be forced to make an emergency landing someplace? If they were in trouble, would I be left alone to handle whatever this mission was?

Chapter 5

Mission: Rescue!

A few minutes after practice got started, Charlie walked back into the gym. He motioned to Bly. As they stood together conferring, I could tell something was wrong.

Bly suddenly turned around and blew his whistle. "Listen up!" he commanded. Everybody stopped as they dropped their basketballs and stood silently still.

"The Kodiak team is in trouble," Charlie began. "Their plane went down about sixty kilometers northwest of here. But..." He couldn't even finish. Everybody was stunned. They all started talking at the same time.

"Are they dead?" asked someone.

"How bad was the crash?" another asked.

"Where are they?"

"Wait a second," said Charlie, holding up both

hands to settle us down. "I understand you're all very worried, but hear me out." We all got quiet again.

"The pilot figured that he had to make an emergency landing," continued Charlie. "They were almost down when their radio went dead."

"So there's a good chance people on board may still be alive," added Bly reassuringly. It turned out Bly himself was a pilot, so everyone figured Bly knew what he was talking about. He explained how the plane was already low to the ground when they last had contact, and how it sounded as if the pilot was doing okay, considering the circumstances.

"We heard no report of an engine out or anything like that," said Bly.

"Let's just hope there was no trouble, they landed fine, and everybody is in one piece," Charlie said. "Whatever happened, we know they're waiting for emergency help."

"We're the closest town to where they may have gone down," added Bly. "Pull that map down, Peter."

I was glad to see a map. Now I knew exactly where I was. Bly quickly showed us where the Kodiaks probably were. "It's up to us to get help out there as fast as possible," he said.

"Call the rescue team," suggested Cody. "They'll handle—"

"The Inuksuk rescue team has gone to help with a plane crash up north," Laurel interrupted.

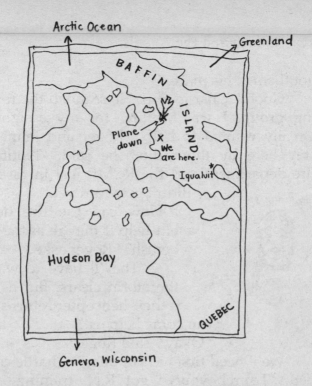

Arctic Ocean

Greenland

BAFFIN ISLAND

Plane down

X
We are here.

Iqaluit

Hudson Bay

QUEBEC

Geneva, Wisconsin

"We'll have to take care of this ourselves," said Charlie. "The faster we get there, the better. So listen up, everybody. We'll need teams to get everything organized. Cody and Malila—you're in charge of food," he instructed. "Go find what you can in the cafeteria." The two girls dashed out in a split second.

"Bly, how about you find Finn Tudlik? The two of you can handle the snow machines." Bly gave him a thumbs-up and quickly got back into his warm clothes.

"And, Bly, get a team of dogs ready for backup," Charlie added.

"We can use my dogs," Bly responded. "Finn's

got them at his place."

"Good," Charlie said. He scanned the remaining group. I was waiting for my assignment. I really wanted to help. "Roger and Jenna, you stay here by the radio," he said. "Notify the fire department and the RCMP, just in case they didn't get word yet."

Charlie giving instructions

"How can the fire department help if they're at the other crash?" Roger asked.

"They'll have to wait till the storm clears. But as soon as their helicopter returns, they can come help us."

"Okay," said Roger.

"We'll need first aid supplies," Charlie continued. "Laurel, you've got R.N. training—that's your job. Peter can help you."

It looked like Charlie was finished. I wanted to say, "What about me?" or wave my arms and jump up and down. But I restrained myself and kept silent.

"Bly and I will navigate on the trip," Charlie said. "We'll decide who else we need to come along."

Now I was jumping out of my skin. I'm sure my angels would want me to go! Why else would I be there? Maybe I didn't know much about the tundra, or snowmobiles, or dogsledding, or saving people in a crash...I suddenly realized that I didn't know *any* of that important stuff. Whoa, maybe I wouldn't be much help after all.

I began to feel completely lost. Why would my angels send me on a mission that I couldn't contribute to?

"Atii!" Charlie commanded.

Everybody hurried to their jobs. I was totally dejected—they didn't need me. The rest of the kids who hadn't been picked all gathered in a huddle, chattering about the Kodiak kids. I had a real hard time not feeling left out.

Suddenly, Finn and Bly came rushing in from the cold, looking very panicked.

"Charlie!" Bly shouted. "I found Finn, but two of the snow machines are down! Only one is working!"

Charlie ran his hands through his graying hair. He was deep in concentration. "Okay. We have to switch to Plan B and use the dogs. How many sleds can we round up?"

"We have Bly's team all ready," Finn answered. "How about your team? It should only take us ten minutes to get them."

"Okay. Go get my team," said Charlie.

"Are two sleds enough?" Bly asked.

"They'll have to be," said Charlie. "We don't have time to go searching for more in this weather." Finn and Bly rushed out to get the dogs ready. Then Charlie turned to me. I held my breath.

"Hannah!" he directed. "You're coming on the trip. In the meantime, Bly and Finn will need help with the dogs. Go see what you can do."

I tore after Bly and Finn so fast that you would have thought *I* had wings.

"*Atii*, angels!"

Atii, Angels!

Chapter 6

Santa's Little Reindeer

Taking care of dogs was the best job I could imagine. I figured it would be like being in charge of a dozen Franks, only these dogs would love snow. I bundled up as fast as I could and ran to catch up with Bly and Finn, who had gone out the back door. Bly took off into the blizzard with a few other guys to get Charlie's dogs. I walked over to Finn, who reminded me of a huge walrus in a red checkered cap.

Don't ask me how, but I could just tell that Finn and I weren't going to get along so well. For some reason, he immediately rubbed me the wrong way. Judging from how he was staring at me (as if I had some sort of disease or something), he probably felt the same way, too. But we were on the same rescue team, so I decided to be nice.

"I'm helping you with the dogs," I said.

Finn stopped and looked me up and down. "Did Charlie send you out here?" he asked.

"Yep," I said. "I'm going with you to help find the plane."

"You?" he blurted out. "How can you help? Do you know anything about *anything* up here?"

I didn't know what to say. All I knew was that I was going because it was the mission my angels had sent me on. I had no idea what they wanted me to do. There wasn't anything I could tell this guy that would make sense to him. Obviously, he thought I was a little kid who would just get in the way.

"Charlie knows why I'm coming," I said.

"I don't want to hurt your feelings, kid," said Finn, shaking his head. "But we can't have a weak link in a chain, if you know what I mean." I knew *exactly* what he meant. Everybody on this mission had to carry their own weight. If one link in a chain breaks, the whole chain falls apart.

"I'm sure I'll be valuable to the team," I said confidently, even though I had no idea what I was going to do.

"Come here, I'll show you what to do with Bly's dog team," said Finn, sighing in frustration. "In the meantime, I'll go talk to Charlie." He turned his back and paused for a moment. Then he turned around and looked me square in the eye. "I'm sorry, but there's no way you're coming, kid—it's *way* too dangerous."

There was nothing to say. I just shut my mouth and followed Finn into a closed-in yard where eight dogs were yipping furiously.

"You get along okay with dogs?" he asked.

"I sure do," I said. "My dad's a vet." But the minute I saw *this* pack of dogs, I wanted to turn on my heels and run back inside for a different assignment—I was terrified! Some were huskies and some were malamutes, but they were definitely *not* cute little white bundles of fur. They looked like wild snow beasts—I think they had more *wolf* than dog in them.

"They know we're heading out soon," Finn explained. "That's why they're so restless." Believe me when I say that these animals were *majorly* stoked to get running.

Finn hung seven leather harnesses over my arm. He kept one to show me how to harness the first dog.

"I'll give you an emergency crash course, uh… What's your name again?" he asked.

"Hannah."

"This is just a quick lesson, uh…Hannah," said Finn. "You'll get more help with the dogs when Bly gets back."

"Sounds good to me," I said, pretending to be more relaxed than I really was. I was *definitely* going to need some help, but I didn't want Finn to know that.

"This is Dasher," Finn said, approaching a

black-and-white dog. He looked like a purebred husky. "The dogs' names are all easy to remember—Bly named them after Santa's reindeer."

"So far so good," I said. At least *something* about my job would be easy.

"First off, you've got to show them who's boss," Finn said. He let out a loud bellow, and the dogs all stopped squirming. "See? When you're authoritative, they respond. Now let's get this harness on."

I watched as Finn fastened the straps under Dasher's belly and around his neck. He told me Dasher was the alpha dog, which meant the leader. Some dogs are natural leaders, and some are followers. I guess they're just like people that way.

"Okay, kid," he said, pulling all but one harness from my arm. "I'll do Comet, you take Cupid." He pointed to a blue-eyed dog that was nearly all white.

I took a deep breath of frosty air and stood up tall. I approached Cupid as if I knew what I was doing. I knew she'd balk if I acted like a scaredy-cat. Besides, there was no way I was going to look helpless in front of Finn Tudlik. He already had me pegged as a "weak link" in the chain.

Harnessing Cupid

I did exactly what Finn had done. I straddled Cupid and got the harness around her neck. Then I went to fasten the back part, but she started skittering around so fast that she kicked snow up into my face. I started getting flustered, which got Cupid even more worked up. Before I could do anything, Finn let out a bellow, and Cupid stopped right in her tracks.

"Don't be afraid to yell, kid," said Finn. "Right from the start, they have to know you're the boss."

"Hey, Cupid!" I hollered as loud as I could.

If I was going to do this job right, I'd have to cop an attitude. I thought about how Ms. Montgomery handles Jimmy Fudge in class—she doesn't let him get away with one bit of fooling around because she knows it would only be the beginning. She lets him know who's the boss, and Jimmy always stays in line.

"I've got to see Charlie for a minute," Finn said. He handed me the rest of the harnesses. "Just keep going...Hilda."

"Hannah," I said for the third time.

Finn quickly pointed to Dancer, Prancer, Vixen, Donner, and Blitzen so I'd know who they were. (He could remember all the dogs' names but not mine.) He left, closing the gate behind him. The dogs couldn't get loose from the area we were in. At least *that* was a comfort.

I set the harnesses onto the snow and took one out for Dancer. I did everything just right. I began to feel pretty proud of myself, but just then,

Cupid decided to run a circle around me, tangling my legs up with her leash. Then Dancer took off in a bolt, and I went crashing down. Dancer careened ahead, hauling me with him.

Dancer dragging me

I tried to hold his leash tight to make him stop. I also tried digging the toes of my boots into the snow. But nothing doing! Dancer was one powerful animal—he dragged me like a sack of potatoes all the way across the yard. I lay there facedown in the snow.

A lot of help I was going to be on this mission.

Chapter 7

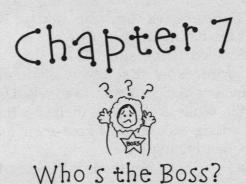

Who's the Boss?

"Hey! What's going on?" Bly yelled from across the fence. Suddenly, I heard a bunch of unfamiliar howls. Wild animals? Before I could get really nervous, I realized it was probably Charlie's dog team. Whew!

Bly walked into the yard and saw me lying there half-buried, pulling my head out of a snow pile. Embarrassed, I struggled to my feet. I wanted to make a joke, but Bly didn't look as if he was in the mood to hear one.

"Where's Finn?" he asked, irritated.

"Talking to Charlie," I said. I decided not to tell Bly what they were talking about. After the way he found me, he'd probably take sides with Finn.

"He should never have left you alone with my dogs!" he said, looking really mad. "Let me finish getting Dancer fixed up," he said as he took Dancer's leash, calming him down.

We finished harnessing all the dogs without another word. Now that Bly was around, they were behaving like perfect little angels. They even stood still while I put on their booties, little doggie shoes that kept their toes from getting injured.

doggie booties

"Let's get them hitched to the sled now, Hannah," Bly said. He grabbed all the leashes and led the dogs outside. "They can't wait to run like a son of a gun," he said.

Charlie's team was ready to go. They were all Siberian huskies and matched almost perfectly. Everybody packed supplies and put them under a plastic cover on Bly's sled while Bly harnessed the dogs. Charlie's sled didn't have plastic—he covered it with a caribou skin.

"That's called an *amiq*," said Bly. "Charlie likes being traditional. He does everything the old-fashioned way, so he uses animal skins and leather straps. He even built that sled himself."

Everybody was very serious as they called out what they were packing.

"First aid kits—two on each sled," said Laurel.

"Blankets and heating packets," called Peter.

"Two-day supply of dog and people food," said Cody.

"My satellite phone," hollered Finn, holding up a big black instrument that looked like it was from *Star Wars*. Even though they were so far out in the wilderness, these guys sure had a lot of equipment.

"Okay, everybody," Charlie said. "The teams are me and Hannah, Bly and Laurel, and Finn will take the snow machine. The rest of you cover the home front."

"If *any* word gets through on the radio, call us immediately on Finn's satellite phone," Bly instructed.

As everybody went to their posts, Finn pulled Charlie aside.

"I can see we need Laurel, since she's a nurse. Bly's got his sled, and he knows the land," I could hear him say. "But I still don't understand that kid—"

"You don't have to understand," said Charlie quietly, cutting Finn off. "We may need her."

"I think we need another able man, Charlie," Finn complained. "She doesn't know anything about the dogs, or—"

"Trust me," said Charlie, putting up his hand to silence Finn. "Hannah's coming with us." Finn turned around and kind of huffed off.

"Get in my sled," Charlie told me. "Laurel, help Hannah get settled."

"What's with Finn?" I whispered when Laurel came over.

"I think he's just being macho," said Laurel. "He'll get over it."

She tucked me into the sled, under the sleeping bags and other stuff we'd packed. I felt like a bug in a rug—only my head was sticking out. Then Laurel snuggled into Bly's sled.

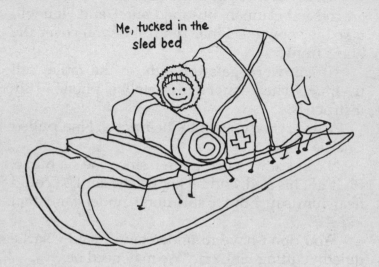

Me, tucked in the sled bed

Charlie and Bly each stood ready at their sleds. Bly put on his lucky Santa hat under his fur hood. Finn revved up the snowmobile. All three men turned on their headlamps, which were bright flashlights strapped around their hoods.

"Everybody ready?" yelled Charlie. We all answered with a thumbs-up sign.

"Can I yell 'Mush'?" I hollered back to Charlie.

"Go ahead," he said.

"Mush!" I hollered in my deepest voice. Nothing happened. "Mush!" I shouted again. The dogs still didn't move.

Charlie and Bly both bellowed some grunt that sounded like *"Ho!"* or *"Hut!"* and the dogs bolted! In seconds, the sleds were speeding along like roller-coaster cars. The snow was coming down nonstop, but we were moving really smoothly. It felt magical—like Santa probably felt with his reindeer on Christmas Eve. As I looked out over the snowy horizon, I just hoped that all the supplies piled around me like Santa's presents would get to the Kodiak kids on time.

Chapter 8

Lemming Land

After two hours of whizzing through the storm, the snow finally started clearing up. For most of the trip, I had pulled my head into my fur hood like a turtle pulling into its shell. Now I could look out and see something other than snow bombarding my face. Every now and then, the moon actually came out to show its frosty white self.

In the light of Charlie's headlamp, I mostly saw the back ends of the dogs. Their curly tails were frozen with ice, but they still kept moving. I had no idea how they managed to keep running all this time. Weren't they tired or cold? They didn't look the least bit fazed by the long and diffi-

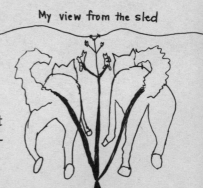

My view from the sled

cult journey we were on. They were truly amazing.

"Trapper Bay!" Finn suddenly yelled. Charlie and Bly pulled the dogs to a halt and hopped off the sleds. The three men trudged to a meeting spot, shoved their fur hoods back, and started talking in Inuktitut. Since I couldn't understand what they were saying, I sat up and observed the dark, cold snowscape around me. I watched some furry snowballs as they scurried across the snow. They must have been animals of some kind. They were about the size of mice. I had no idea what they were.

"What are those little things?" I called over to Laurel.

"They're lemmings!" Laurel yelled back. "Aren't they cute?"

"Lemmings?" I repeated. "Aren't they the Pied Piper animals who follow their leader off a cliff into the sea and kill themselves? Aren't they... like...really stupid?"

This is the actual size of a lemming — cute, huh?

Laurel burst out laughing. "I think that's an old wives' tale, Hannah!"

I had always pictured lemmings as nasty and dirty rats. But from here, they looked sweet, like little snow hamsters. I wanted to get out of the

sled and examine the critters up close and per-
sonal, so I started to push the sleeping bags and
other stuff off of me.

"Hannah!" Laurel yelled. "Stay in the sled!"

"Why?" I whined.

"I just heard them say we're ready to leave,"
she answered, pointing to the three men. "We're
at the coast of Trapper Bay. Charlie thinks the
Kodiaks' plane isn't far away."

The men were gazing at the sky as Charlie
pointed over at the Big and Little Dippers. I
guessed that they were getting their bearings by
looking at the North Star, which is in the handle
of the Little Dipper.

Out of absolutely nowhere, a sudden chill hit
me and raced through my body like a cold electric
shock. I was rattled from the bumpy ride, and my
nose and toes were freezing, but this chill was
something totally different. It was almost as if an
angel message was delivered *through* my body. I
couldn't hear it, but I could see it. It was like a
picture in my head, like a dream with my eyes
wide open. I saw thin ice, breaking up. It looked
extremely dangerous. There were little icebergs
floating around like islands on the frigid Arctic
water.

Am I seeing a vision of the plane the kids were on?
I thought to myself. *Did they go down on the ice and
crack it to bits?* I shook my head no. I didn't want
to believe it—that would be just too horrible a
situation.

Just then, Charlie shot a questioning look at me. He trudged over to the sled and stared deep into my eyes for several seconds.

"Danger?" he asked. "Did you say 'thin ice'?" But I hadn't said a single word! It was as if Charlie had heard what I was thinking. *Very* spooky. Just then, Finn revved up and sped on ahead.

"We have to get moving," Charlie said to Bly. "And watch out for the ice."

For the next few minutes, I felt so cold and frightened that I wished I was back home chasing my tail with Frank. But I didn't have much time to think miserable thoughts, because suddenly, the vision I had was right before my eyes. But this time it was for real!

Charlie brought the team to a screeching halt so fast that the dogs nearly crashed right into each other. Then he and Bly jumped off their sleds and raced ahead on foot as fast as they could. The beams from their headlamps pierced through the darkness.

"Finn!" they were yelling. *"Finn!"* Their voices were swallowed up by the howling, fierce winds. I pulled my flashlight out of my backpack. Through the flurries, I saw water reflected in the dark with hunks of ice floating on top. It was exactly like my dream. But then I saw Finn's snowmobile drifting off on a huge sheet of ice.

Finn was nowhere in sight.

Chapter 9

Ice Palace

This time, Laurel and I jumped out of our sleds.

"Stay right there!" Bly yelled at us. "Don't move one inch! We've got fragile ice here!"

Then we heard a terrible wail. It was Finn.

"Help!" he bellowed like a wounded walrus. "I'm over here!" Bly and Charlie found him and lifted him to his feet.

"Are you all right?" Charlie asked him.

He was drenched in icy water, growling and shivering. "I saw the bl-black ice, and I th-thought it was a few feet thick," he said. "I should have t-tested it first…" He was hitting himself in the head. It looked like he felt really stupid.

Finn the Walrus man

"Hey, we're just glad you're in one piece," said Bly. "It's a good thing you're well insulated."

"But check out my sno-go!" he moaned through chattering teeth. We all looked, just as the snowmobile was drifting away on its ice raft. The wind was blowing fiercely, pushing Finn's machine farther and farther out of reach.

"So long!" said Bly, trying to keep Finn's spirits up.

"Now what?" Finn asked. "I can't travel by sled. I know you and the dogs can't handle my extra weight."

"We better call for help before you get frostbitten," said Charlie. "Where's your satellite phone?"

Finn reached inside his soaking-wet parka. "Oh, no!" he screamed. "I can't believe this! It must have flown out when I jumped off the snowmobile! It may have sunk." He started rumbling around in the snow, all mad, trying to find the phone.

Laurel and I were still standing right beside our sleds. She shook her head miserably. What were we going to do? I had a gut feeling Finn was not going to find that phone. It was too cold to pull out my journal, but I mentally listed our choices as if I was writing in my "Actions and Consequences" section:

Action #1: Leave Finn and go ahead.
Consequence: He might die from the cold before we
    could get back to save him.
Action #2: Make Finn run alongside the dogs.

consequence: We'd end up going so slow, the Kodiak
 kids would be frozen by the time we got to the
 plane (if they weren't frozen already).
Action #3: Get the snowmobile, somehow, before it has
 sunk.
consequence: We'd be on our way to completing the
 mission.

Obviously, Action #3 was the only way to go. But
how could we get that snowmobile back? Before I
could come up with any ideas, I heard a distant
drumming. Was someone coming? Was it the kids
from the plane signaling us?

"Laurel!" I called. "Do you hear that drumming?" She looked at me like I was nuts. But I still
heard it getting louder and louder. It was just like
the drumming I'd heard back home on Geneva
Lake!

"Charlie!" I yelled. I'm *sure* Charlie would
have heard it, but he was too busy with Finn. I
closed my eyes to focus. *Thump! Thump! Thump!*
A faraway voice joined the drumbeat. It sounded
like the whistling wind.

"Rush...sh...sh...Hurr...rry..." it said. I
could tell it was Lyra, my
musical angel, giving me a
message. She was telling us to
hurry to the kids! I listened for
the *thump, thump, thump*ing and
her windy voice one more time

just to make sure. No doubt about it, she was definitely telling us to rush. Then I suddenly heard a walloping holler. It was Finn, all miserable, screaming about his lost snowmobile.

"First the phone, now my snow machine!" he complained. "She's going down, Charlie! She's sinking!"

I didn't open my eyes to look. It wasn't that I didn't want to, it was more like I couldn't. My eyes were pasted shut. I kept hearing that loud, steady drumbeat. "Hurr…rry…Rush…sh…sh…"

"Look, Finn!" Bly suddenly yelled. "Your machine's turning around! It's…coming this way!"

"Holy smokes!" Finn hollered. "What in blazes is going on?"

"How can this be?" yelled Bly, awestruck. "She's sailing *against* the wind!"

Now my eyes popped open to see Charlie, Bly, and Finn all staring at the snowmobile. It had spun around, facing them, its headlight glaring bright in the darkness. The machine was practically flying toward Finn on its ice raft!

My windy angels

"Well, I'll be a blue-nosed lemming!" Bly yelled. "The wind's completely turned around!"

What they didn't see was the invisible force behind the wind. I knew it was my angels back there pushing the wind so we could get that machine and save the kids! We couldn't waste any time fooling around—and my angels made sure we didn't. Charlie turned to me and nodded as if to say thank you. I had no doubt—*he* knew exactly what was happening. *How* he knew, I had no idea.

"What's going on, Charlie?" Finn was yelling as he waited for the snowmobile to get close enough to grab. "How can the wind make a complete 180-degree turn like that?"

"That's why Hannah is on our trip," Charlie said.

Finn scratched his head in wonder. "Well, I just don't get it. How did Hilda...I mean... Hannah...?"

"Don't ask me any questions," Charlie told Finn flatly. "Just tell Hannah thank you."

Finn looked totally perplexed. I could tell he didn't want to thank me. He probably thought I had nothing to do with it (which, actually, I didn't—but my angels did). But he gave in anyway.

"Thanks," said Finn. He was actually polite. "Thank you, Hannah," he repeated. Wow, he even got my name right, too. Maybe Finn was starting to come around.

"Now grab that machine, and let's get you dried off before you get frostbitten!" said Charlie.

"Where in the world can he dry off out here?" Bly asked.

"Follow me," said Charlie. "We've got to make a short pit stop."

Laurel and I snuggled back into our sled beds. I was happy to be back in our little nests because the wind had picked up and was really wailing. Finn was soaking wet, but he got back on his machine. It made me cold to my bones just to *look* at him. The dogs took off as Charlie led the way.

Soon, I saw something in the distance. At first, it looked like a hill, but as we got closer, I realized it was an igloo! As we sped toward it, it looked bigger and bigger—more like several igloos all attached. Maybe it was an apartment complex or some kind of ice palace.

Suddenly, people began to gather outside the igloo. They must have spotted our headlamps. As soon as we stopped, the people made sure that Finn got right inside. They all seemed to know Charlie and welcomed him in Inuktitut. They laughed and patted him on the back and were all really friendly to the rest of us, too.

Laurel, Bly, and I fought the wind as we pulled a few supplies from the sleds.

"I've never seen a real igloo before," I said to Laurel. The wind caught my voice and carried it far across the tundra.

"That makes two of us," she shouted, cupping her hands over her mouth. "I didn't even know we Inuit built igloos anymore."

"Some people still build them," Bly yelled as we made our way toward the door. "It's temporary housing, a winter camp where we can fish, hunt, and live the traditional life. But they're not actually called igloos."

"I guess I should have known that," said Laurel, a little embarrassed. "What *are* they called?"

"*Illu* is the Inuit word that means any kind of house," Bly explained. "The word for snow house is *illuvigaq*." It sounded to me like he was saying "eee-loo-vee-gock."

"How did Charlie know this place was here?" I asked.

"Haven't you noticed? Charlie knows everything," Bly said. "He never ceases to amaze me."

Inside, the snow house was awesome—just like a magical ice palace. There were four rooms, including one with a big dome that Bly said was a hall for dancing and a special porch for the dogs to protect them from the wind.

In a way, I was glad Finn had to dry off—it meant I could warm up, too. But as soon

Ice palace

as I thought that, I felt tremendously guilty. After all, the poor Kodiaks were out there someplace in this freezing wind, waiting to get rescued. At least I *hoped* they were waiting.

Chapter 10

Blubber for Supper

Charlie introduced us to everyone in the snow house, but there were way too many people to remember. I did catch the names of two boys my age: Robert and Kook. They were really nice and offered to help me get the dogs settled. So we went outside and pulled the dogs out of the screeching winds. We led them through a corridor whose walls were made of snow blocks and into an enclosed kennel. The roof was open, but the snow walls kept out the wind.

"Good thing the dogs didn't go down in Trapper Bay," said Robert.

"I'll say!" I agreed. "Finn could handle the frostbite better than the dogs would."

"I'm surprised the ice wasn't frozen," said Kook.

"So was Finn!" I said. "I guess he hit the one

place where it was thick enough."

We got the dogs comfy by taking their harnesses and booties off. They still seemed a bit restless. We realized that they must be pretty hungry. "They deserve a special feast!" Robert exclaimed.

I followed the guys to the side of the snow house, where there was a pile of stones half-buried in snow. It looked like a sturdy little man.

"That's so cute! It's an *inuksuk*, isn't it?" I yelled. I was all proud of myself for knowing what it was—it was the same stone man as the one on the Inuksuk School banner.

"It marks our cache," said Robert. He didn't seem to be excited about my Inuktitut knowledge like I was. But now I had another new word to master.

"It marks your *cash*?" I asked. "You bury your money in the snow?"

Kook burst out laughing. "Not our *cash*. Our c-a-c-h-e, Hannah!" he said. It was like saying "blew" and "blue," or "hair" and "hare." They sound exactly the same but mean very different things. I had no idea what a cache was.

"A c-a-c-h-e is a place where you hide valuable things, like food for hunting," Robert explained.

"And the *inuksuk* marks it, so when it gets covered in snow, we don't forget where it's buried," said Kook.

"That's pretty cool, Kook," I said as we started digging around in the snow by the *inuksuk*. There was a deep hole underneath.

"The food stays nice and cold in there," said Kook.

"It's just like a refrigerator," I said. Robert and Kook started pulling bundles out of the cache.

"Seal...fish...walrus," they called as they tossed rock-hard frozen pieces toward me. I could just picture feeding this stuff to Frank. He'd turn up his little spoiled nose. He likes his dog food in bite-sized pieces at *perfect* room temperature. I don't think he'd take too kindly to an eight-pound side of walrus.

We cradled the frozen food in our parkas and carried it into the dog kennel through the snow block tunnel. The snowmobile was parked in the corner, and all sixteen of our dogs were lying next to it. The minute they smelled dinner, they got all excited. I quickly got down in a crouch (which, I know from my dad, is the friendly way to be around dogs) and thanked them all for their hard work. I called every one of them by name. I'm not sure I matched the right dog with the right name, but I did my best.

Here are all their names really fast (I was practicing them on the sled ride to see how fast I could say them without

Me, Kook, and Robert feeding Conan

taking a breath): Dasher, Dancer, Prancer, Vixen, Comet, Cupid, Donner, Blitzen, Conan, Mush, Cherokee, Cream o' Wheat, Midnight, Ursa Major, Ursa Minor, and Petunia. Whew!

Kook and Robert then gave them their food, and they absolutely loved it.

"The fish gives the dogs beautiful coats," said Robert.

"And the walrus and seal give them strength," added Kook.

By the time we got the dogs fed, it was time for us to eat. We went back in by the heater—which was called a *qulliq*, where everybody else was sitting around—and warmed up. I tossed my socks and mittens in the drying basket and snuggled up in a fur blanket. As I enjoyed the warmth from the *qulliq*, I remembered the ice

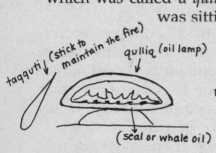

taqquti↓ (stick to maintain the fire)

qulliq (oil lamp)

(seal or whale oil)

shacks and heaters on Geneva Lake back home. I bet they don't use seal oil for their heater fuel!

We had *maqtaaq* (which is pronounced muktuk), and it was a real treat for everybody, even though it's thick pieces that are cut from frozen whale skin! I know it sounds totally gross, but it actually tastes really good. I ate blubber for supper—and liked it! Kook told me that it gives you lots of strength for journeying out into the cold.

Robert was laughing at me when I took my first bite because I looked pretty scared. But after I ate my piece, I pulled out my oranges and chocolate chip cookies and passed them around.

While we munched on *maqtaaq* and chocolate chips, Finn kept checking his clothes to see if they were dry yet. Everybody was talking in Inuktitut. Laurel leaned over to translate a few things for me. "Charlie's asking if they've got a snowmobile here."

"Do they?" I asked.

"They sure do," she said. "It sounds like a couple of us are leaving right away." Just then, Bly jumped to his feet and motioned to Laurel to do the same. Obviously, they were going now.

"But, Charlie," I said. "How will they know where the plane is?" I had figured my angels would guide us to wherever the plane had landed.

"I have a general idea of where it probably went down," Bly cut in. "And Charlie has the same feeling."

"We'll be okay," Laurel assured me. "We have no time to waste."

"We'll get a head start, and maybe I can even get the pilot's radio going and let the RCMP know where the plane is," said Bly.

This was the second time I had heard the RCMP mentioned, and I still had no idea what it was. I quickly asked Kook in a whisper to explain it to me. Turns out it's the Royal Canadian Mounted Police—you know, the Mounties on horseback, who wear the red coats. Except in the Canadian Arctic, they wear whatever keeps them warm so that they can concentrate on helping people in trouble, like the Kodiak kids.

"We'll take off as soon as Finn is dry," Charlie said. Finn let out an ornery growl. He was still disgusted with himself. He knew that he was making everybody wait for him. *So who's the weak link in the chain now?* I said to myself.

After Bly and Laurel left, everyone was silent for a moment. I think they were all wishing that the Kodiak kids were all right. At first, I was a little fidgety, but eventually I enjoyed the quiet. As I looked around the room, I noticed that all the faces were golden brown. I pulled my journal out of my backpack and started to write a story about me being born an Inuit baby. I'd have dark brown eyes and a round face with smooth skin, like soft leather, and straight black hair. The Arctic wind would have screamed across the tundra on the day I was born, but I would have slept cozy and warm inside my parents' fur blankets. I would hear old tales about the Arctic seals and whales from my grandparents. When I got bigger, I would learn to watch out for polar bears, or maybe even to hunt them for food to put in my cache. I would also learn how to collect dry caribou droppings to make fires and how to build a little snow house. I would also learn to sing.

I thought of the singing part because two women began singing in the middle of my daydreaming. They were facing each other, and they made noises from their throats that echoed back and forth in each other's mouths!

"It's called 'throat singing,'" Charlie explained. I wouldn't have believed it if I hadn't seen it with my own eyes. I made a pledge to try it with Katie when I got back home.

Chapter 11

Poison Pawprints

I thought I'd check on the dogs while Finn kept on drying out. The snow had stopped, the wind had died down, and the moon was as bright as all those fluorescent lights at Dude's Super Foods. I thought the dogs would probably be sleeping after such a strenuous day. Not a chance! They were romping around like puppies.

After playing with them for a brief moment, I settled onto a snow ledge and pulled out my flute. It was so cold that I felt like the mouthpiece would freeze my lips if I wasn't careful. I played a little "Claire de Lune," which is a song about the moonlight. Then I tried out the telescope my angels had left me for the mission. I focused on Orion, the hunter, with the three stars around his waist.

I wished David was with me. He's my other

best friend, and he knows the name of every single constellation. He's told me that the huge star
at the top of Orion's right shoul-
der is a thousand times bigger
than our sun. He says it's so
enormous that if it was our sun,
it would burn the earth right up
and reach all the way to Jupiter.
Imagine that!

I always feel very tiny
under all the stars, like a little
flicker of a person in an awe-
somely huge universe. Suddenly,
Dasher came over and nudged my
kamiik. He was all jittery. He kept
nudging and then stumbled backward. Then he
came back and nudged me again.

Stargazing

"What's the matter, boy?" I asked. "You tired?"
I felt like my mom when she's talking to me.
"Hannah, you're tired, and you need to go to bed."

Then I noticed that *all* the dogs were acting
weird. They were stumbling around and pushing
each other, behaving like keyed-up little kids. I
walked toward their huddle and let out a ferocious yell to remind them it was me, Hannah the
Boss, and I was in charge.

"Ho! Time for a story, you guys!" I commanded. "Sit down and listen up!" I was all set to
tell them about the cow jumping over the moon
and the little dog laughing. I guess I was inspired

by the gigantic Arctic moon up above. But they didn't settle down for a single moment.

Then I noticed the prints. There were zigzag trails of little green pawprints. Were my angels giving me a message? I got off my ledge, bent down, and examined the prints. There were a lot of them.

I hadn't paid any attention before to the fact that all the dogs were in a huddle. But now I checked it out. I could see that they were eating food or something, shoving each other away to get at it first.

"Hey!" I bellowed.

Dasher looked up immediately. His fur was pale lavender from the moonlight, but his face was dyed bright green all around his mouth. I burst out laughing. He looked pretty funny, like he'd been drinking lime Kool-Aid. I walked around the edge of the dog huddle, trying to get a better look. Then I noticed that they all had green mouths! What in the world were they eating?

"Move!" I yelled in my toughest mush voice. They didn't budge—whatever they'd found must have tasted really good.

I started to wriggle through the pack. I was very careful since I knew they still didn't trust me. I was also very aware of the wolf blood that was in some of them. I made a lot of loud noises and kept my hands out of reach. Finally, I got to where they were drinking. A pool of lime green liquid had spilled onto the snow. I had no clue what it was.

I didn't want to stick my finger next to all those dog teeth, so I stuck the end of my *kamiik* into the green pool. I wiped some onto my glove, lifted it to my nose, and sniffed. It smelled like detergent. I touched the very tip of my tongue to the edge of my glove. It burned! Why would the dogs like this? But then again, if *maqtaaq* was a people treat, maybe this was some sort of Inuit dog treat.

I stood and thought for a minute. In my gut, I knew something was terribly wrong. The more I *really* looked at the dogs, I could see their eyes were glazed over. They were staggering into each other, dizzy, and now some of them could barely stand up on all fours.

Dasher's wild eyes

What was going on? Finn's snowmobile was parked right next to the dogs. Now I could see that the green liquid seemed to be dripping from underneath the machine. And the burning in my mouth was getting worse. There was no way this green stuff could be good for these animals.

I rushed back through the dog pack and tore into the igloo.

"Charlie!" I yelled. "The dogs are eating something weird!"

"What is it, Hannah?" Charlie asked.

"Something green," I said. "I think it's dripping from the snow machine."

He leapt to his feet instantly. So did everybody else.

"Are they acting like crazy maniacs?" Charlie asked me as he shot out the door. Three more people, including Finn, rushed out behind him.

"Yes!" I said, alarmed. "Their eyes look funny!" Now that the grownups were so worried, I was even more scared than before. I hurried back outside.

Suddenly, the whole place felt like an emergency room. Charlie and Finn took charge immediately. They began barking commands at the dogs and yelling at all of us to pull them away from the pool.

"Are you nuts? Get out of there!" Charlie bellowed at Dasher.

"Hannah, where are the harnesses?" Finn hollered. I raced back in, grabbed the harnesses off the hooks, and got the dog to Finn. He harnessed up Dasher and tied him up far away from the snowmobile.

It looked like a tornado scene in a movie. Every person had a dog by the leash and was struggling to tie that dog up. We were all harnessing and yelling and yanking, and not one dog wanted to come. They were ferocious, acting like wild wolves, nipping at their masters and howling to get back to the green goo. They loved that stuff.

Meanwhile, Charlie was kneeling in the snow, touching the liquid.

"It's just what I thought," he said miserably.

"It's antifreeze, ain't it, Charlie?" Finn hollered. He sounded panicky.

"Yep." Charlie was hanging his head like it was the end of the world. "I didn't expect this at all," he said quietly.

"Antifreeze?" I asked, pulling Cherokee by the collar. Actually, he was pulling *me*, right back toward the green pool. I wasn't sure what antifreeze was. I only knew we put it in the engine of our minivan. "Is that bad?" I quickly realized that it must be bad or everybody wouldn't be in such a panic.

"It's poison, Hannah," Finn whispered to me. "Deadly poison from my sno-go."

A chill ran through me that was much worse than one from the cold or snow. I felt my jaw harden and freeze. Everything was total havoc. Finn was frantically moving the snowmobile back against the wall. Charlie was kicking a pile of snow over the pool of antifreeze. People were hollering at each other about what to do.

I just stood there, frozen, in the middle of it all. I've never felt so guilty in my whole life. How could I be so careless? I had been sitting around stargazing while right under my nose, the dogs were lapping up *poison!*

Chapter 12

Aurora Borealis

Charlie looked into Cupid's eyes. Then he checked inside her mouth.

"How much do you think they lapped up?" asked Finn, joining him.

"Too much," said Charlie. "We can try to treat them, but it doesn't look good."

Charlie knew what Finn was thinking. "It's not your fault," Charlie said to him.

"Can he heal them?" I asked Kook. Since Charlie was a medicine man, I thought maybe he could give them an herb or do a special dance or something. I felt desperate. I was sweating underneath my parka.

"We're way out on open tundra," whispered Kook. "I don't know if—"

"Go get salt," Charlie commanded, interrupting us. Kook and I followed orders and dashed inside.

"Salt!" I shouted. "We need salt!"

"Why?" asked Robert.

"The dogs drank antifreeze from the snow-mobile," I cried.

"Oh no! Not the dogs!" said Robert. "Quick! We have some salt stored here."

Robert got the salt and dashed out the door. Kook turned to me somberly. "This will make them throw up the poison. But..."

I didn't like the tone of his voice. "But what?" I asked.

Kook was silent, staring beyond me toward the door.

"You better just get out there and help," he said after a moment. I turned to go, and then I saw what Kook had been looking at. Charlie was standing in the doorway, his face washed out and his eyes intense.

"Any chance of the salt absorbing all that poison?" asked Kook.

"Not a chance. It will slow down the process for a while, but these dogs will need medicine."

"Can you...I mean...I heard you were a... medicine man, and...maybe you have powers to...?" I stammered.

Charlie looked right through me as he turned to walk back out the door. "I can't do anything," he said quietly. My heart sank. I couldn't believe that there was nothing we could do for these animals.

Suddenly, Charlie waved his hand for me to follow, like when he first met me in the blizzard. The stars sparkled in the black sky as I walked behind him. The snow squeaked under my feet. For some reason, I couldn't help but feel like a little kid in big trouble.

Charlie took a tall stick that was leaning up against the snow house and stabbed it into the snow. He began to sing, very quietly, in Inuktitut. Maybe he was singing a song to forgive himself in advance for the cruel way he was about to punish me for killing the dogs.

He raised his arms to the stars in the east. Then he walked to the south side of the snow *illu*. I squeaked along behind him, not saying a word. I was frozen on the outside because it was so cold, and I was frozen on the inside because I was so afraid. My tears were streaks of burning ice on my face. Charlie sang toward the south, the west, and the north, until he made a full circle.

He pulled the stick out of the snow. I was sure he was getting ready to hit me hard over the head with it or do something else I felt I deserved. I'd killed the dogs, and without them, we couldn't get to the plane. If we didn't get to the plane, everybody would freeze. It would be my fault if the Kodiak kids died, too.

Charlie raised the stick upward toward the northern sky. I flinched.

"Put your arms up, Hannah!" he commanded. "Way up!"

"What are we doing?" I asked him.

"You know what we're doing," he said. "Talk with your angels *now*," he said.

What? Charlie knew about my angels?

He began chanting and singing again, as if he had his own angels to talk to. I felt a rush of relief. I realized he wasn't going to punish me after all.

I did just as Charlie had said and called out to my angels. I talked right out loud, just like Charlie was doing.

"Aurora, Lyra, help us!" I said desperately through my tears. "Demi, Lori, please! Tell us what to do."

Charlie was singing loudly now. I tried to match his volume, but I couldn't through my crying. When I looked up, the night had turned as bright as day—and the sky was green. True! It was a deep green, and the snow was turquoise. My mouth dropped open as I looked above the horizon and saw awesome, shimmering ribbons of light dancing in the air. They were greenish at the top, and the bottom edges were pink and gold. It looked like one huge, silky curtain fluttering through the stars.

"Are those the northern lights?" I whispered to Charlie.

He didn't hear me. He was standing with his stick held high in the air, whistling. And the more he whistled, the closer the lights seemed to move toward us. The sparkling curtain began to open right down the middle. I blinked a few times and stared at the bright lights. Something came out of the curtain, flying at an incredible speed. Could it be...my angel Aurora?

Aurora Borealis ?

Chapter 13

Skunk Muffin

What an awesome entrance! Aurora looked like a shimmering rainbow with wings. I wished I had my telescope with me so I could get a closer look at her. She spread out her wings, and different colors flew down from her and touched the ground.

Suddenly, I felt fine. I was totally calm, as if everything would work out. I glanced over at Charlie—he was still whistling. The more he whistled, the closer the curtain of light came and the brighter it got. Now all I could see were colors: red, violet, yellow, and green. It was so bright that I had to close my eyes for a second. It was magical—like we were *inside* a rainbow.

Charlie stopped whistling. I opened my eyes. Aurora was gone. But the northern lights were still shimmering away. I let out a big sigh. I still had the feeling that everything would be fine. I knew something wonderful had just happened. But what? I mean, the dogs were still poisoned, we didn't have the medicine to cure them, and we had only one broken snowmobile to get us to the Kodiak kids.

"Did you see Aurora?" I asked Charlie.

"The aurora borealis," he said quietly, with great respect. "The northern lights, always a wondrous spectacle."

"No, I mean my angel—" I started to say.

He put up his hand to silence me. Then he pointed to the horizon just beneath where the aurora borealis was still putting on a show. There was a silhouette walking toward us. It was a person, but I couldn't tell if it was a man or a woman.

I squinted. It was dressed all in fur, wearing cross-country skis. It looked like a man from the way it walked. In fact, it looked a lot like...No! This was impossible! I held my breath and kept watching. The person slowly skied over to us and pulled back the hood on his parka. I saw familiar green eyes and brown curly hair. I thought I was going to have a heart attack!

"Dad?"

"Huh?...What the... Where the...?" he said. He was frowning, and totally confused. He was

Dad ?

staring at me with his mouth hanging open. It looked like *he* was going to have a heart attack, too.

"Dad?" I said again. Either this person was my father's long-lost twin, or I was in the middle of a very wild dream. Maybe that little taste of antifreeze had tweaked my brain cells around.

I shook my head really hard. Would I wake up now and be back, trudging through the snow in Geneva? I looked again. My dad was still standing there. I guess I was totally stunned and overexcited, because at that moment, I got the hiccups.

"Skunk Muffin! What on earth is going on?" my father demanded. Then I knew for sure it wasn't a dad double. Who else would call me that name? This was my very own father standing in Baffin Island snow, with his vet pack on his back.

"*Hic!*" I said. I couldn't believe it!

"Come with me," said Charlie, grabbing my dad's arm. "You and Hannah can sort this out later. Right now, the dogs need you."

"Dogs?" my dad repeated, stumbling along while Charlie dragged him to the other side of the snow house. "Hannah?"

"*Hic!* I'm coming, Dad!" I hollered, following them as fast as I could.

"Will somebody tell me what's going on?" my dad yelled.

Even though it was tremendously weird seeing him on one of my angel missions, it was pretty funny watching him. He had completely flipped out.

"I was just helping Sasha give birth to her new pups," he was blabbering. He was gawking back and forth from the northern lights to me to Charlie to the snow house. "What *is* all this? Where on earth *are* we? And how did…?"

"It's an emergency," Charlie interrupted quietly but firmly. "These dogs are full of antifreeze, and we need your medicine."

"Antifreeze? That's ethylene glycol poisoning," he said, suddenly serious.

"That's right," Charlie agreed. As we entered the snow kennel, the dogs were weaving and staggering all over the place with shiny, glazed-over eyes. A few of them had passed out. I was afraid to ask if they were still breathing. The minute my dad saw them, he quit worrying about where he was and got right to work.

"How much did they swallow? When did they drink it? Show me the antifreeze. Did you give them any medicine yet?" He kept asking Charlie more questions.

"Good," he said after Charlie filled him in. "Salt was the right thing to do. What else do you have on hand?"

"Nothing," said Charlie. "That's why you're here."

"The antifreeze goes right to the dogs' kidneys. It will shut down their functioning within a few hours," said my dad. "We need 4-methylpyrazole."

I had no idea what my dad was talking about. Four *what?*

"You've brought medicine with you, yes?" Charlie asked calmly. "You're an animal doctor, right?"

"No and yes," my dad said. "I *am* an animal doctor, but I was totally unprepared for this call. I don't carry chemicals like that with me all the time."

"*Hic!*" I said.

"Without 4-methylpyrazole," said my dad, "I'm afraid these dogs will be dead by morning." He looked around at the frozen tundra. "I don't suppose there's a hospital around here?"

Charlie shook his head. "No, Doc. And even if there was a hospital, the only way to get there is with the dogs."

I looked at Charlie and then at my dad. My heart sank. I wanted to help, but all I could do was stand there and hiccup.

Chapter 14

Husky Hospital

Something happened to me at that very moment—I began to lose hope. I looked up through the open roof and watched as the northern lights faded away in the dark sky. The show was coming to a close. But there was one bright yellow-gold spot left, just where I had seen Aurora.

I heard my dad talking to Charlie.

"I need IVs and filters, too. I don't carry..." As he spoke, I just kept staring at that glowing spot in the sky like I was hypnotized or something. Then I felt a tug. It wasn't my hair—my hood was covering my head. But I felt a distinct pull and shove on my back, as if somebody had reached in and was grabbing stuff out of my backpack.

I felt like my whole body was surrounded by the last golden glow of the northern lights, and

A tug on my backpack

then it dawned on me. Yes! Could it be that somebody was putting something *into* my backpack? I quickly dropped the pack onto the snow. It made a soft thump as I tore off my mittens, not caring about the freezing cold. I ripped open the flap and examined the contents of my backpack.

"Da—*hic!* Da—*hic!*" I took a breath. *"Daaad!"* I finally managed to scream. My dad spun around, startled by my outburst.

I couldn't get a word out—I just kept hiccuping. So I shoved my backpack into my dad's hands and pointed inside. His eyes got as huge as two green Arctic moons.

"How in the world…?" he started to stammer.

"Perfect," said Charlie. He knew immediately what was going on. The angels had supplied me with everything my dad didn't have in his bag. There were bottles of fourwhatevers and IVs and filters!

Just then, Finn walked out and spotted my dad. "Where are all these strangers coming from?" he said, amazed. "They just keep multiplying!"

"No time for explanations," Charlie said. He was talking to both Finn and my dad. "Let's just get to work."

Now the ice kennel had really turned into an emergency room. For the next few hours, my dad was head doctor of Husky Hospital. We all did whatever he told us, with no questions asked.

"First of all, let's get these dogs in where it's warm," he said. The dogs were so tired that they were easily led inside to the heaters. My dad took the supplies from my backpack and set them on an ice shelf. He lined up the IV tape and needles and medicine. Together, we had every single thing he needed.

"Charlie, keep the dogs calm so they won't be too scared," my dad said.

"Sure thing," said Charlie. He started humming a sweet hymn.

"Hannah, you can help me hold the dog's leg while I put the needle in," my dad said. He

Me, Petunia, and my Dad

showed me how to hold Petunia's leg up off the ground while he found a vein to stick the needle in. He pulled out the needle and taped on the little IV tube, and then I set Petunia's leg back down. We worked really quickly, moving from one sick dog to the next. Charlie talked and hummed softly to each dog while my dad gave them shots and taped on the IVs. Soon all the dogs had medicine dripping into their veins.

Then my dad set up a schedule so that everybody would take turns watching the dogs through the night to make sure they were okay. I helped put my dad's supplies into his bag and then collapsed by the fire between Cupid and Conan. I was completely exhausted.

"You think the dogs will be all right, Doc?" asked Charlie.

"I sure hope so," said my dad. "You seemed to catch it quickly enough. That's important in cases like this."

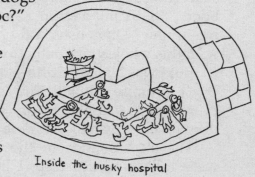

Inside the husky hospital

"How soon can they run again?"

"We'll give them another round of shots in the morning," said my dad. "But it'll take at least twelve hours."

"Twelve hours!" hollered Finn. "Those kids will be frozen dead in twelve hours!"

"What kids?" my dad asked. I had completely forgotten that he didn't know about anything that had happened. Finn proceeded to fill him in, while I lay between the dogs, fighting off sleep.

I closed my eyes and listened to all the sounds around me. Finn was telling his story, Charlie was humming to the dogs, and Kook and Robert's family were talking softly in Inuktitut.

"Thanks for coming, Doc," Finn said.

My dad started to laugh. He hadn't cracked a single smile since he'd arrived here because everything had been so hectic and serious.

"It wasn't as if I volunteered for the trip!" he said, chuckling. He nudged me with the tip of his boot. "So, Skunk Muffin...are you ready to clue me in now? Obviously, you had something to do with this whole...uh...situation."

But I was already drifting off.

"I promise I'll tell you tomorrow, Dad," I mumbled. I was hoping my angels would come up with an explanation for me by then.

The slow sounds of the Inuktitut language were lulling me to sleep. I listened to the long *eeeeee*'s and *oooooo*'s and *aaaaaa*'s. They moved up and down, rhythmic as the ocean waves. I remember imagining that I was drifting off to the song of a whale—a far, soft lullaby.

Chapter 15

Fireworks in the Sky

It was still night when I woke up. Then I remembered that it's practically always night during the Arctic winter. The dogs were gone. I was the only one by the heaters. I didn't know if I'd been sleeping for a minute, an hour, or a whole day.

"Let's go, Hannah!" my dad called from outside. I quickly got bundled up and ran outside. I couldn't believe what I saw! The dogs were harnessed up, with their booties on. Everybody was ready to go!

"The dogs are all better?" I asked.

Amazingly, things had seemed to work themselves out while I was asleep. The dogs healed unbelievably fast. (No doubt my angels had something to do with that!) And I didn't need to go through a whole long explanation with my dad. My macho buddy Finn had actually come to the rescue. He'd told my dad that Charlie was a medicine man and had certain magical powers. Finn said that Charlie probably got my dad and me spirited off to Baffin Island to save the dogs. Finn also said that he didn't know how these things worked, but neither did my dad, so he seemed satisfied with that explanation. Well, sort of, anyway. What a relief! Now I could just focus on my mission and get to those poor kids.

"How do we know where the plane went down?" my dad asked.

"Charlie has a sixth sense," said Finn. "He found *you*, didn't he?"

We took off, bumping across the wide-open tundra once again. I was getting used to it now. I kept my eyes peeled for foxes and Arctic hares scooting across the snow. And, of course, lemmings. Then I had a sudden surprise—a white owl flew down out of the darkness and circled over our heads.

"Charlie!" I yelled, pointing. "That's what I saw when I was lost in the blizzard! That was the shining thing circling above me in the storm when you found me!"

"An *ukpik*," Charlie shouted back.

"What?" I called.

"A snowy owl. We call him *ukpik*."

"You mean that owl has a name?" I thought it was pretty strange that a wild animal would have a name, like my dog, Frank, or David's ferret, Squirt.

"All snowy owls are called *ukpik*," said Charlie as he pulled the dogs to a halt.

"Oh. But how could an owl fly in a storm?" I asked him. "And how could the same owl have followed us all the way here?"

"You ask a lot of questions, don't you, Hannah?" said Charlie, smiling.

Just then, Finn and my dad pulled up next to us.

"We're going to follow the white owl," said Charlie. Finn nodded like that made perfect sense. My dad, on the other hand, looked at the two of them like they were nuts.

"What do you mean, follow the owl?"

"Don't worry, Doc," said Finn. "Charlie has a different way of navigating, but he's always right on target."

My dad looked very perplexed, but I don't think it bothered Charlie and Finn. With a few "*Ho*"s and "*Hut*"s, we were off again following the *ukpik*. He flew straight ahead, while Charlie and Finn steered around the areas that looked too bumpy or icy.

Soon I spotted something through my telescope that looked like an animal in the distance. The strange thing was, though, it wasn't white. I thought all the Arctic animals turned white in the winter. I squinted harder. It looked familiar, but I couldn't tell exactly what it was.

When I looked back up in the sky, the *ukpik* was gone! I got a little worried, but I guess I didn't have to since it wasn't my job to run the sled. Charlie kept going straight on toward the dark, familiar-looking animal. Finally, we were close enough for me to see that it wasn't an animal.

"Charlie!" I yelled, turning around in the sled. "It's an *inuksuk!*" It was a stone-man marker, like the one that had covered the food cache.

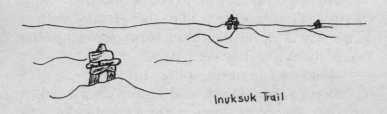

Inuksuk Trail

"You're tipping my balance!" Charlie yelled back. "Turn around!" But it was too late. The sled was heavy on one side now, and it tipped over enough so that the first aid kit rolled out. The dogs noticed right away and stopped running. Those huskies are pretty smart—they started turning around, looking at me with their blue eyes like they wanted an explanation for why I had slowed them down.

"Sorry," I told Charlie. "Sorry to you guys, too," I told the dogs.

"Okay," said Charlie. "Just pick up the stuff that fell out, and we'll get going again."

"At least we didn't tip all the way over," I said, climbing out to pick up my mess.

"Just quit moving around in there," said Charlie. "We're almost to the plane now, and we can't lose any more time."

I didn't waste another minute. I got the stuff, tucked myself back in, and stayed perfectly still. But I noticed something weird.

"Charlie! The *inuksuk*—it's gone!" I screamed.

"Ho!" Charlie shouted to the team, ignoring me. But the minute we started up again, I saw the *inuksuk!* Then I saw another and another. It was a trail of *inuksuk* markers that seemed to be leading the way to...

"Look up ahead!" Charlie yelled. I stood up to see. It looked like the Fourth of July. A red flame soared into the sky.

"They're sending up a flare!" my dad shouted.

"They see our headlights coming!" hollered Finn. "It's them, all right! We've tracked down the Kodiaks!"

A flare!

Chapter 16

Angels, Angels Everywhere

As we sped over the next hill, I could see the plane, a bunch of people in parkas, and a little snow house. Behind the people, fireworks started bursting in the sky. They weren't just flares, they were actual fireworks!

"Guess who's doing that?" yelled Charlie. Before I could get an answer, I peered out and saw Bly. He was dancing and jumping around with his Santa hat on in front of the colorful display. He was celebrating our arrival.

"He brought fireworks with him?" shouted Finn, shaking his head.

"That's Bly for you!" said Charlie.

Kids began to rush out to us, yelling and waving their hands in the air. I saw pictures of bears sewn onto their parkas—it must have been the Kodiaks' symbol.

"Hey, over here!" they were yelling. (Like we could possibly miss them!) When our sleds pulled up near a burning campfire, everybody began talking at once. There were 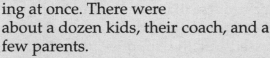 about a dozen kids, their coach, and a few parents.

"The pilot's hurt," a kid screamed.

"The radio was smashed!" said another.

"You have any food?"

Laurel immediately got the extra first aid kits from our sled. Bly came over to help now that his fireworks show was over.

"Is anybody critical?" asked Charlie.

"No, mainly just cuts and bruises and a little frostbite. Three of the kids knew CPR, so they did a great job with a kid who'd stopped breathing," Bly said.

The CPR kids started telling us the whole story of the emergency landing, and how they'd pulled a few people out of the wreck and got the unconscious kid breathing again. They were pretty proud of themselves.

"The pilot's in the worst shape," Laurel cut in, talking to Charlie. "He has a slight head injury."

"Where is he?" asked Charlie.

"Inside the *illuvigaq*," said Laurel. "I think you should take a look at him."

"I was just about to," said Charlie, following her to the snow house.

The rest of us started pulling the supplies out of the sleds and giving them to the kids. It was like we had two concession stands set up—me and Bly at one, and my dad and Finn at the other. I was beginning to feel like one of Santa's helpers as everybody swarmed around us.

As we passed out the supplies, they told us how they'd been burning anything they could find on the plane to keep the fire going. They'd survived for twenty-four hours on hot Gatorade, energy bars, and the oatmeal cookies that one of the moms had baked for the trip. One of the kids had cut a hole in the ice and managed to catch a couple of fish.

"We've been starving!" someone moaned.

"Then feed your face!" yelled Bly, tossing the boy a food bag. The boy opened it and started throwing beef jerky, water bottles, and apples to everybody. They acted kind of like they were on the basketball court.

"Pass it here!"

"Over this way!"

"I'm open!"

They were intercepting each other's apples and tossing beef jerky like they were sinking baskets. For being in such a serious situation, they looked like they were actually having fun!

"How'd the snow house get here?" I asked.

"They built it!" said Bly. "They did everything they were supposed to do—thrive, survive, and stay alive!" I couldn't have said it better myself.

"So the radio's down?" Finn asked Bly.

"It *was* down," said Bly.

"But he got it going again!" a bunch of kids yelled at once, pointing at Bly.

"You fixed the radio?" Finn asked, impressed.

"Sure did!" said Bly. "Help is on the way!"

He put an arm around my shoulder, and we walked over and hung our arms around my dad and Finn to form a circle.

"We have a pretty good team here," said Finn.

"I got the radio fixed, you guys arrived with the food, and Charlie and Laurel are helping the pilot," said Bly. "And now we've got angels flying in any minute."

"Angels?" I said. Bly knew about my angels, too?

"RCMP angels. Red Cross angels. You name the disaster, they're on their way to help!" he said.

Little did Bly know how many angels had already flown in. The ones coming in helicopters were just the backup.

Chapter 17

Ukpik

After our emergency work was done, I went off to see how they had built the snow house.

"Finn, why don't you go with Hannah while I play some b-ball with this lousy, second-rate team!" Bly teased. Howls and boos came from the Kodiaks. They started running around in the snow with Bly, using apples for balls.

"Quit being a ball hog!" Bly yelled. "Pass it over here!" He was having a grand old time. It was obvious that Bly believed the expression "Laughter is the best medicine."

Finn, my dad, and I went over to the snow house, where some snow bricks were piled up.

"They didn't just use any old knife," said Finn. "They had to use what we call a 'snow knife.'"

He pulled a long, curved knife out of a pile on the ground and handed it to me.

"We have different names for different types of snow," he said. "Falling snow is called *qanik*. Snow on the ground is called *aputi*. You want to use the hard-packed snow to make blocks for building."

I decided to give it a try. I sliced through the thick snow like I was cutting a loaf of bread. Six slashes and I had a snow brick! Finn lifted it up and set it next to the others in the stack.

"Dad, you want to try?" I asked as I gave him the snow knife.

Cutting snow blocks

"Sure!" he said. He was much faster than I was. He slashed a brick out in no time and stacked it on top of mine.

Just then, Charlie came out of the snow *illu*.

"How's the pilot?" my dad asked.

"He's going to be okay," Charlie said. "But I'm glad the Red Cross is coming. He could use a good bed right now."

"So could I!" said Finn, yawning. He was right, we could all use a good bed. After all, it *had* been an extremely long night.

"So, you building a hospital over there, Doc?" Charlie asked my dad, pointing to the snow brick.

"That's a great idea, Charlie," said my dad, laughing. "It'll be my winter office!" He cut another snow block and fit it next to the others. It was starting to look like a wall now. Dad was really getting into it.

I noticed that Charlie was wearing a carved owl that was hanging from a leather string around his neck.

"Charlie!" I screamed, pointing. "That's an owl, isn't it?"

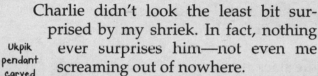

Charlie didn't look the least bit surprised by my shriek. In fact, nothing ever surprises him—not even me screaming out of nowhere.

Ukpik pendant carved from whale-bone

"Yes, it's a snowy owl," he said. "Come here a minute, Hannah," he said, motioning to me to follow him. "You're very curious about the *ukpik*, aren't you?"

"Yeah, I saw it twice and thought it was incredible both times. Is it real?" I asked. "Or is it like a mirage?"

"Hannah," Charlie said quietly. "What if I asked if your angels were real?"

"They're not a mirage, if that's what you mean," I said. I didn't like thinking that my angels were some kind of imaginary spirits, or like the magic rabbits you pull out of a hat. "They're *definitely* real."

"So if they're real, does that mean everybody believes in them?" asked Charlie.

"No..." I said.

"And if not everybody believes in them, does

that mean they don't exist?" asked Charlie.

"No..." I said. "They do exist. I hear them. Sometimes I even see them."

"Fine," said Charlie. "That's just my point. Your angels make sense for you, right?"

"Yes," I said.

Charlie smiled. "Then I don't need to ask you about your angels, Hannah," he said. "And you don't need to ask me about the *ukpik,* or shape-shifting, or anything else. What's important is that we each did whatever we could to save these kids."

"You're right," I said. "That *is* what's important."

He took the pendant from around his neck and put it over my head. "This is for you," he said.

"You're giving this to *me?*" I asked.

"Yes," he said. "I appreciate what you and your father did. I'm forever grateful that your angels sent you this way."

"Thank you so much, Charlie," I said, running my fingers over the owl's face.

"Your father calls you Skunk Muffin, doesn't he?" asked Charlie, smiling.

"Sometimes," I said.

"What does it mean?"

"Nothing, really," I said. "He just thinks it's cute."

"Well, now I have a special name for you, too.

When I think of you, I'll remember you by this name."

Charlie told me my special name, but I can't tell you what it is because it's actually a secret. I'll give you a hint, though. It's a name that means I bring messages and healing with me on my angel trips. You know what? I'll write it down for you in angel code. If you figure it out, just don't blab it around, okay? Let's try and keep it a secret.

My secret name

"Angels headed this way!" my dad suddenly hollered.

"Angels?" I asked. "What do you—"

"Red Cross helicopter. At least one, maybe two," he said.

"Vehicles are coming across the hill, too!" hollered Finn.

Everybody started hooting, whistling, and waving their arms. Help was coming from all sides.

Angels, angels everywhere!

Chapter 18

Some Sleepover!

The whole area was suddenly overflowing with people and machines and noise. Emergency medics were taking a look at the few who were injured, and the rest were grabbing their stuff, which had been blown all over. My dad and I got herded onto a helicopter. Before we took off, I looked back at the crash scene one last time. A warm feeling came over me. *Everything worked out*, I thought to myself.

On the way back to Inuksuk, I saw the whole landscape we had crossed by dogsled from a brand-new perspective. White animals—like Arctic hares, lemmings, and foxes—were scurrying across the flat snow. I didn't see any caribou or bears, but I knew they were there someplace. I couldn't believe how much faster it was by

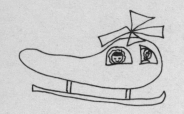

helicopter—incredibly soon, we landed outside the school.

Peter, Cody, Mary, and Malila came out to greet us. Peter had a bullhorn.

"It's the heroes!" he announced, his voice loud and blaring.

"We heard all about it on the radio!" cried Malila.

"Who's this?" Peter asked.

"It's my dad," I said. My dad looked at me like he was all confused again.

"How do you know these people?" he asked.

"Let's not talk out here in the cold," said Malila. "Come inside." *Thank you, Malila*, I thought. (I didn't want to deal with another explanation, especially in front of the kids.)

The gym was set up like an emergency shelter. There were tables with crackers, cereal, fruit, and milk on them. There was also a nurse's station with two emergency medics waiting for the plane passengers to arrive. There were even cots set up, with blankets and pillows.

"We pulled out the cots so we could have somewhere to sleep last night," said Malila.

"It looks like you guys had a giant sleepover," I said.

"We sure did," said Malila. "When the snow stopped, some parents were able to get through and drop off food and blankets. We stayed up really late, listening to the emergency radio and..."

The end of her sentence was drowned out by the noise of the next helicopter arriving. Laurel came in with some of the Kodiaks. She quickly joined the medics at the nurses' station. Once each kid was checked for injuries or frostbite, they went straight to the basketball court. My dad headed there, too, along with a few other parents.

Instead of playing their big game against one another, the Mighty Nanuks and the Kodiak kids practiced together like they were one team. During the practice, in between dribbling and shooting, the Nanuk players were asking all about the details of the Kodiaks' adventure.

In the background, past the voices and the basketball practice, I began to hear drums. *Thump, thump, thump,* like a heartbeat. I knew it was time, so I ran over to give Laurel a big hug.

"I've got to go," I said as she bandaged the forehead of one of the players.

"Well, before you do, I have to ask you about the *inuksuk* trail, Hannah," she said.

"You mean the markers that led the way to the plane?" I asked her. I was wondering about them, too—the first one had disappeared right before my eyes.

"Yes, those markers," she said. "They appeared out of nowhere! Bly and I couldn't believe our eyes. Without them, we might *never* have found these kids," she said as she smiled at the Kodiak kid she was doctoring up.

The drumming was getting really loud now. I heard a faint voice. "Rushsh...sh...sh..." it whispered. I remembered Lyra, out on the tundra, telling me to hurry and get to the kids.

"It was you, wasn't it, angels? You put the *inuksuk* trail there?" I asked. Suddenly, a soothing sensation came over me, as if to tell me I was right. I knew it!

"What were you just saying?" asked Laurel.

"I have to go, Laurel," I said. "Charlie should be able to tell you, though!"

"*Tavvauvusi*, Hannah!" Laurel said, smiling. I knew it meant good-bye, so I tried it, too.

"Tah-vow-voo-see, Laurel!"

I knew I'd be back home any second because the drumming was getting incredibly loud. I figured that I wouldn't get the chance to say good-bye to Charlie, Bly, and Finn. But what I cared about most was whether my dad could come back with me. I mean, if he couldn't for some reason, like if my angels didn't know how to get him back...*then* what?

I glanced over at him to see if he heard Lyra's drums. I couldn't tell, though, because he was too busy playing ball. I raced onto the basketball court, grabbed him by the arm, and quickly yanked him outside into the freezing, dark snow.

"Hannah, what in the world..." he began. But suddenly, I couldn't hear him anymore. The drums were so loud that they drowned him out. And that was it.

We were gone.

Chapter 19

New Babies

I was back in a flash. And I was *so* relieved to see that Dad had made it back, too. But then I suddenly realized I would have to tell him all about my angel missions. I began to get a little nervous—I wasn't exactly sure how he was going to take it. After all, he is my dad, and he cares about my well-being. And sometimes my angel missions aren't the safest trips out there.

Dad was squatting down next to a snow white husky and her four newborn pups.

"You did a great job, Sasha," he said to the mom dog. Kyle Jacobson's grandmother was standing beside my dad, beaming with happiness.

"Thank you so much, Dr. Martin," she said, watching the squirming little pups with pride. "Just look at those darling babies!"

"Sasha is a little worn-out, since she's older," my dad said. "But she'll be just fine."

Mrs. Jacobson looked over at me. "Why, Hannah!" she exclaimed. "I didn't even see you come in! Aren't they adorable?"

The blue-eyed snowballs

"They sure are," I agreed. The puppies looked like furry snowballs with soft blue eyes.

"Oh, hi there, Skunk Muffin!" said my dad. "What are you doing here?"

I watched his face closely. I didn't see an ounce of remembrance of the angel trip. He was perfectly cool and calm.

"I...I just thought I'd go for a hike in the snow," I stammered. "And I knew you were here on a call."

"Well, I'd say Sasha needs some time alone with her new pups now," said Dad, standing up. He strapped his cross-country skis on.

"You're walking, Hannah?" he asked me.

I nodded.

"Well, see if you can beat me home!"

He skied off with his backpack on his back as Mrs. Jacobson waved good-bye. I tramped through the snow as fast as I could, but Dad got home way before I did. When I walked in the door, he was already sitting by the fire, giving Frank a treat. The note I'd left for him before my mission began was in his hand.

"Your note says you were off on an adventure," he said. "So did anything exciting happen, Hannah?"

I dropped my backpack on the floor and started pulling off my boots. I didn't know what to say. Did my dad really not remember our trip? Things were beginning to look bright.

"Uh…as a matter of fact, I *did* have an adventure," I said.

"Want to tell me about it?" he asked as he poked the logs on the fire.

Just then, Mom came in to join us by the fire. "So I'm glad to see the two of you made it back from the blizzard safe and sound," she said. She had brought us hot chocolate with extra marshmallows.

"Sure did," said my dad, taking a sip from his mug. "The Jacobsons' dog had four beautiful new pups. And Hannah was just going to tell me about her snowy adventure."

I watched my dad's eyes closely. *Nothing.* Not one glimmer of recollection. I think he really didn't remember!

"Ummm, well…I made a snow angel on the lake," I said. I had no idea how to continue. I was about to say that I had built a snowman or something like that, when Mom cut me off.

"Where did you get that pendant?" she asked, pointing to my neck. "It looks like it's carved out of bone!"

I looked down. It was the snowy owl from Charlie! I was so happy the angels had sent it back with me, but now I'd have to figure out an explanation—and quick!

"It *is* made of bone," I said. "Whalebone. Isn't it cool?" *Think fast, Hannah,* I told myself. *Change the subject, quick.*

"Is it an owl?" my mom continued.

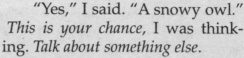
Did you say "ukpik"?

"Yes," I said. "A snowy owl." *This is your chance,* I was thinking. *Talk about something else.*

But then Dad said something that caught me way off guard.

"I think it has something to do with…an *ukpik*," he said.

Ukpik? My hot chocolate went down the wrong way, and I started choking.

"What's an *ukpik?*" asked my mom when I was done coughing.

"It's a snowy owl that lives on the Arctic tundra," my dad answered matter-of-factly. He settled back in his chair with his cocoa in hand. I was waiting for him to say next that his innocent little daughter had exposed him to this rare animal when she decided to whisk him away to Canada on a dangerous mission. Then I was waiting for my mom to go absolutely nuts. Basically, I was expecting a pretty ugly sight. I was about to come clean when Dad interrupted.

"I was reading about it in one of my nature magazines," he said earnestly. "They have a lot of incredible animals in the Arctic. Maybe one day, we can all bundle up and take a family trip out there."

Suddenly, a small rainbow that looked a lot like a miniature version of the northern lights appeared above my parents' heads. Only I could see it. I immediately knew it was Aurora sending a message. She was telling me not to worry—*Our secret is still safe and sound!*

Way to go, angels, I thought to myself.

Hiccup!

(Uh-oh! Here I go again!)

THE INUKTITUT ALPHABET
by Hannah Martin

THE 3 VOWELS:

◁ A
(sounds like "ahh")

Δ I
(sounds like "eee")

▷ U
(sounds like "ooo")

THE EASIEST CONSONANTS:
(You add them at the end of a syllable like a little tail.)

⟨ P	∪ G	⌐ S	ℓ V
⊂ T	L M	⊂ L	ᖑ R
ᑲ K	ℯ N	⅄ J	

CONSONANTS COMBINED WITH VOWELS:
(Each sound is one letter, like the sound for "ki" would be written down as "P.")

⟨	pa	Λ	pi	⟩	pu
C	ta	∩	ti	⊃	tu
ᑲ	ka	P	ki	ᑯ	ku
∪	ga	Γ	gi	⌐	gu
L	ma	Γ	mi	⌐	mu
ℯ	na	σ	ni	ᓄ	nu
ᒐ	sa	⸡	si	⸡	su
⊂	la	⊂	li	⊐	lu
⅄	ja	⸜	ji	⸜	ju
ℓ	va	∆	vi	⸜	vu
ᖅ	ra	ᖕ	ri	P	ru

I'VE GOT MAIL!

I just got a letter from Laurel! I guess she wants me to practice my Inuktitut. I already figured out what the words say. (It makes a great secret code—David will love it!) If you want to try it, I'll give you a few hints.

Hi, Hannah!

Guess what's been happening in ᓄ ᐵᶜ?
The minute you left, an ᐅᖕᐱᖕ flew inside the gym and we had quite a time chasing it back out the door. Yesterday, we found out ᐸᑐᐊ is going to have babies! Today is Charlie's birthday, and we made ice cream out of ᐊᐳᑎ to surprise him. Want the recipe?

ᑕᐸᐅᕆ, Laurel

P.S. Charlie says "good journeys" to ᑐᓚ ᒥᑭᔪ.

HINTS:

Inuktitut has only 3 vowels: eee (i), ooo (o), ahh (a). There aren't as many consonants as we have in English, either. The symbols combine one consonant with each vowel., like ki, ku, ka and ti, tu, ta. And check this out: ki, ku, ka = ᑭ ᒃ ᑉ. And ti, tu, ta = ᐱ ᑐ ᑕ. It 's the same symbol, just turned backwards or upside-down! Clever, huh? So Katie's name would be kaiti, or ᑉ ᐃ ᑎ. Get it? Ka-i-ti.

The hard part for me was the tiny symbols that get added, like when you square a number in math. (Hey, Ms. Crybaby—it's called an exponent! I remembered!) Actually, those tiny symbols are just consonants added on. All the consonants by themselves are written tiny, and higher than the rest of the word. For instance, Inuit would be: i-nu-i or ᐃ ᓄ ᐃ. But then you want to add the "t" at the end. So you stick a little "t" or a ᶜ on for a tail, and you get: ᐃ ᓄ ᐃ ᶜ

By the way, ᑐ ᓗ ᒥ ᑭ ᔪ (which is pronounced tuluga mikiju) is my secret name in Inuktitut!

See you later!

COOL ARCTIC STUFF

Antifreeze—Fluid you put in your car to keep the engine from freezing up in the cold. It's bright green and has a sweet taste that animals seem to enjoy. It's very poisonous and can be fatal. (Thank goodness my dad showed up!)

Arctic Animals—All the animals of the Arctic are white so their enemies can't see them. These include snowy owls, polar bears, foxes, Arctic hares, and even lemmings (the *only* rodents in the world who ever turn white!). The other cool thing is that their hairs are actually hollow, so they capture air, which somehow warms them up in winter. Other Arctic animals I didn't see on this trip are caribou, seals, walruses, and whales.

Art—For centuries, Inuit people have carved Arctic animals and people out of natural materials like driftwood, whalebone, soapstone, walrus tusks, and caribou antlers.

Aurora Borealis (uh-ROAR-uh boar-ee-AL-iss)—Otherwise known as the northern lights, it's an awesome glow that fills the whole sky with color at night. It's caused by sunlight skimming across the cold northern atmosphere, making ribbons of red, pink, purple, green, and gold. Some Inuit people (like Charlie) believe if you whistle at the aurora, it will come closer to you.

Cache—This sounds like the word *cash*. In the Arctic, it's a hiding place that's dug into the frozen ground. Robert and Kook's cache was a natural refrigerator where they stored fish, seal, whale, walrus, and caribou meat.

Dogsledding—It's one way to get around in the Arctic—you ride on a sled pulled by dogs. If you want to be a musher (a dogsledder), you need a team of dogs, a sled, and a lot of equipment. For instance, the dogs need harnesses, lines to pull the sled with, and booties; you need warm clothes, a headlamp, a compass, and a radio. And take lots of food and water for all of you!

Drums and Dances—Inuit drums are usually made of stretched caribou skin and are played for all kinds of celebrations. Inuit people often perform drum dances for special occasions, like welcoming a friend for a visit.

Games—There are a lot of traditional Inuit games. The blanket toss is the one I played—you get tossed on a massive sealskin blanket. I didn't try the one-foot high kick, but I heard you try to jump-kick a hanging sealskin ball high over your head, then land upright again on one foot. There's also a two-foot kick, which looks impossible!

Hamlet—It's a small town. Inuksuk is the hamlet that my angels sent me to on this trip. (But you won't find it on a map!)

Huskies—Most dogs who pull sleds are pure husky or part husky. Some people also use malamutes. Bly says that all sled dogs live to run and there's always a leader—the alpha dog. And there's always a slacker. That's the dog who *pretends* to pull the sled but really just runs along letting everybody else do the work. (Sort of like Jimmy Fudge when Ms. Crybaby divides us into work groups.)

Igloo—This is really *illu* (eee-loo), the Inuit word for "house." A dome-shaped house made of snow blocks is called an *illuvigaq*, which sounds like this: eee-loo-vee-gock. (Try saying *that* three times fast!) Not many Inuit people live in permanent snow igloos anymore. Mostly, they build igloos for hunting and fishing. Like the ice houses in my town, you probably wouldn't choose to live in one full-time.

Inuit—The name of the native people who live in northern Canada (and in other places, too, like Alaska). Don't use the old word, *Eskimo*, because it can be insulting to Inuit people. *Eskimo* is a Cree Indian word that means "eaters of raw meat." I sure wouldn't like to be called "eater of pepperoni pizza." Would you? There's a lot more to me than what I eat! The right way to say *Inuit* is Eee-noo-eet.

Inuksuk—It's pronounced eee-nook-sook and means "like a human." It's a little stack of rocks that looks like a standing person. Inuit people use them to mark certain places, like a trail or a food cache or a dangerous area.

Medicine Man—A person who has gifts that include healing people's bodies and spirits. A true Inuit healer is very quiet about these abilities and never calls himself (or herself) a "shaman" or a "medicine man." Only fake medicine men would use those words to describe themselves.

Midnight Sun—It's the Arctic summer sun, which stays above the horizon constantly, including in the middle of the night. I'd never sleep! My trip was in winter, so it was the opposite—it was night almost all the time!

Nunavut (Noon-uh-voot)—This is the newest territory in Canada, just formed on April 1, 1999. (That's my birthday, too!) It's one-fifth the size of Canada. The word means "our land," and

Nunavut is governed by the Inuit people so their own culture can continue and grow. Baffin Island is the site of Nunavut's new capital, Iqaluit (Eee-kal-uh-weet).

Outpost Camp—This is an isolated place where Inuit families live a traditional life, hunting, fishing, and trapping to get their food and clothing. Robert and Kook's snow house was an outpost camp.

Permafrost—In freezing climates, the top 200–2,000 feet of ground, which never thaws—not even in summer! Brrrr!

RCMP—The Mounties, or the Royal Canadian Mounted Police, which is Canada's national police force. Sometimes they ride on horseback, but up in the Arctic, they mostly drive sturdy vehicles and dress really warm!

Satellite Phone—This kind of portable telephone can be used in *really* remote places (like Arctic outposts) where cell phones won't work.

Singing—Inuit people have always loved to sing. A lot of songs tell stories; sometimes a song is given to somebody else as a gift. (Isn't that cool?) The throat singing I heard is an old Inuit tradition. The singers stand face-to-face and sort of warble like birds. The warbles vibrate with each other, and it sounds awesome. When Katie gets back, maybe she'll try it with me.

Transportation—Besides dogsledding, you can get around in a small airplane, seaplane, snow machine (also called "snowmobile" or "sno-go"), ATV (all-terrain vehicle), kayak, or umiak (a kind of rowboat). Don't look for regular cars or roads in the Arctic tundra, except maybe in the middle of towns.

Tundra—This is the flat plain in the Arctic where it's too cold for trees to grow. I didn't see anything but snow, snow, and more snow. But Charlie says that when the snow melts, there are lichen and moss and little wildflowers everywhere.

A LITTLE DICTIONARY FROM MY TRIP

The Inuit people speak Inuktitut (eee-nook-tee-toot). Here are some Inuktitut words I wrote in my journal:

Aputi (ah-poo-tee)—Snow on the ground.

Atii! (ah-tee)—Let's go!

Ikajunnga (eee-kah-joon-gah)—Help!

Ikuala (eee-kwah-lah)—Fire.

Illu (eee-loo)—House.

Kamiik (kah-meek)—Cozy boots made from sealskin, caribou skin, or canvas.

Maqtaaq (muk-tuk)—Chunk of whale skin and blubber you eat frozen or boiled.

Nanuk (nah-nook)—Polar bear.

Qanuippit? (kah-nwee-peet)—How are you?

Qujannamiik (koo-yon-nah-mee-ick)—Thank you.

Qulliq—An oil lamp.

Taqquti—A stick that's used to maintain a fire.

Tavvauvusi (tah-vow-voo-see)—Good-bye.

Ukpik (ook-pick)—Snowy owl.

Make sure to read
ALL of the exciting
Hannah adventures!

Hannah #1: Mission Down Under

For my first mission, the angels send me to Australia, where I help my new friend, Ian, track down some really mean poachers. The trouble is, we aren't always sure who's getting hunted—the animals or us!

Hannah #2: Searching For Lulu

Now I'm in Kenya, where I need to find a special medicine for a girl named Mchesi who's really sick. According to the angels' messages, I'm looking for a healing green pearl—but I'm running out of time!

¡Hola! (Hello!) from sunny Mexico, where the angels have sent me on Mission Numero 3! X marks the spot where my new friend Luis and I suspect some greedy thieves have hidden an important treasure. But now I have another sneaking suspicion: Is *Luis* hiding something important from *me*?

Hannah #4:
Notes from Blue Mountain

Guess where the angels have sent me now? To the Appalachian Mountains—right here in the U.S.! One minute I'm listening to scary stories in a fire-lit cabin, helping Annie and her friends get ready for the big autumn festival—and the next I'm searching for Annie's brother, who's been kidnapped!

Hannah #5: Saving Uncle Sean

Well, it's raining (again) here in beautiful Ireland, the Emerald Isle. And you know what? The whole place really does look green. But I don't have time to look at castles and amazing scenery. The angels need me to help Molly Ryan, because her uncle is in *really* big trouble!

Hannah #6: Mardi Gras Mix-Up

Everyone loves a great party. Especially *me!* And what better place to party than Trinidad at Carnival time? But my new friend, Frankie, isn't having much fun. At first I thought the angels wanted me just to try and cheer him up, but my mission is even more important than that...